Dust from Stars

Pamela L. Seay

Printed in the United States of America

Author: Pamela L. Seay

Cover design by Pamela L. Seay

First Printing: September 2023

ISBN: 978-1-7359822-4-3

As a star blazes through the sky it leaves a trail of dust far behind.

Part I: Sam

1

Beep... Beep... Beep... Beep...

"Is it necessary for me to still be hooked up to this machine."

The nurse ignored me as she rolled her eyes and left the hospital room.

I laid in this uncomfortable hospital bed for almost a whole day with only the sound of the heart monitor echoing in the cold delivery room.

Although the summer's in London were mild, I was sweating so much that one of the nurses laid a cold compress on my forehead.

I couldn't believe I had given birth a day ago to a daughter named Sadie.

I didn't get a good look at her at first as the female nurses swaddled her in a small blanket and excitedly ran to the other room to present my newborn to Sasha while leaving me alone with the doctor.

Annoyed, the doctor had to call out for one of them to stay and assist him because I had some complications.

I was surprised Sasha even made it in time for the birth

as he was usually in London. He spent most of the time in the waiting room, occasionally coming in to help me get our daughter to feed.

Beep... Beep... Beep... Beep...

The beeping was driving me crazy. I reached behind me to unplug the annoying monitor when suddenly a nurse in her late 50s with kind eyes entered the room holding my daughter wrapped in a fresh clean white blanket.

"We finished with the final test and I thought you would want to hold her before you're discharged."

She placed her in my arms.

"Thank you."

Each time I held her it surprised me how tiny she was.

One of her small hands escaped from the tightly wrapped blanket. I placed my finger into her palm and she instinctively enclosed it while looking up at me with her bright green eyes.

I could definitely see Sasha in her and strangely she resembled my mom as she raised her eyebrows in a way that my mom did when she was upset with me.

At that moment nothing around me mattered, just her.

But, that moment didn't last long as the room was suddenly flooded with nurses, Sasha, and the public relations entourage.

"I need you to change into this outfit for the paparazzi as you and Sasha exit the hospital with the baby." Renae a public relations person Sasha demanded I hire shoved a blue wrap dress on a hanger into my hand.

Sasha smelled like a Saturday night as he leaned over to kiss my forehead.

"How are you?" His eyes squinted with concern as I laid in the hospital bed balancing holding our daughter and the dress.

"Sam we need you to hurry and get dressed." Renae reached down and pulled our daughter from my arms and handed her to Sasha. Then, she threw back my blanket from my legs and guided me to the bathroom.

She practically shoved me through the door leaving me alone in the small white restroom.

Although the doctor gave me pain medicine, I was still sore and could barely pull the hospital gown off without wincing in pain.

After tying on the wrap dress I glanced at my reflection in the mirror. I barely recognized my pale, swollen face with red blotches on my cheeks. My auburn hair was messy and thinning in the middle but, I was too worn out to fix it.

Knock.. Knock.. Knock..

"Are you almost ready?" My head began to pound with the sound of Renae's voice.

I opened the door and she rushed in with a brush and a pair of blue ballet slippers.

"Let's get you fixed up."

She laid the slippers in front of me and as I slid my feet into them she began brushing my hair into a low ponytail.

"Okay that looks better. Put these shades on, it'll hide the puffiness in your face."

I looked up and Sasha stood behind Renae with two security guards bewildered at my appearance.

Renae stepped out the room to speak with one of the guards to ensure our driver was parked in front of the hospital for our exit.

Sasha cautiously moved towards me.

"Are you okay? We don't have to leave just yet if you're not ready?" His deep British voice and dark kind eyes relaxed me and made me feel safe. This was something I had not felt from him in a long time.

"I just want to go home."

He nodded and Renae came booming into the bathroom again.

"It's best if Sam is holding the baby and Sasha make sure you wrap your arms around them. And, remember cover the babies face, we agreed to an exclusive photo reveal for BritPress magazine."

Sasha gently placed our daughter in my arms and wrapped a pink silk shawl over my shoulders to help me hide her face.

"Okay, let's exit this way."

Two additional security guards guided us through the brightly lit hospital corridor towards the exit.

The hospital staff and a few patients stood against the walls staring at us with wide eyes of disbelief and admiration.

"The driver is parked to the right of the steps."

Sasha wrapped his arms around my shoulders and pulled me close to him. I looked up at him and he smiled reassuring me that everything would be okay.

"We're ready! Let's open the doors!"

The doors flung open and a flood of flashing lights blinded me making the shades over my eyes useless.

2

With the entertainment media watching and commenting on my weight and waiting to see if I would bounce back to being beautiful and fit again put a lot of pressure on me to diet and workout.

Sadie and I went to a televised Christmas musical special Sasha did with other iconic musicians and the cameramen recorded me in the audience.

Afterwards, the mean comments all over social media about my puffy face made the need for me to lose the baby weight was Renae's top priority.

With the major fashion weeks for London, Milan, and Paris starting that February I needed to get back in shape, quickly.

As Renae constantly told me, the more beautiful I am after having a baby the more money making opportunities I will have. And, I needed the money.

While the $150,000 a month I got from Sasha was a lot, with the cost of maintaining my appearance with cosmetic procedures and designer clothes, the money was almost all spent by the end of each month. So, Renae found me paying opportunities to cash in on being married to an iconic rock star.

To uphold Sasha's image, she insured that all of the jobs I did were the most prestigious.

I only worked with the top designers, make up and skincare brands, and a few luxury store openings. And, sometimes Sasha came with me to these events which made it even more special.

But, as the weather began to warm and the summer touring season was looming closer, Sasha wanted me to focus more on staying home to care for Sadie and managing the estate while he was away to promote the band's upcoming album and tour.

I stared at Sasha's suitcase sitting on the floor in front of his closet door.

The few times he was home, he would leave his suitcase in this very spot and disappear into his office on the first level of the estate.

I opened the hard shelled black suitcase and began sorting the contents into piles for laundry.

Over time, I realized how difficult it was for him to transition from life as a rock star on the road to being a normal human with a wife and child.

It always took him a few days to acknowledge our existence when he returned. And when he did, he usually spent most of his time complaining, working on music, or his endorsement deals and scotch whiskey business.

I placed the dirty clothes into a laundry basket and set it just outside the bedroom door for the housekeeper to collect.

His shoes, toiletries, and jewelry I placed in their proper places within his large dark wood paneled walk-in closet.

Our daughter Sadie and I have grown accustomed to

life with just the two of us.

On the occasional sunny day we'd have the driver take us to the beach in Brighton to play in the sand and shop along the boardwalk.

Sometimes, people recognized me, but no one ever bothered or harassed us.

It took a while for me to adapt to my new life in West Sussex, but with Sadie, I definitely appreciated the slower pace here and privacy of the large estate.

The massive property felt like my own world.

I could go days without seeing anyone but my little Sadie.

At almost a year old now, she was responding more to me and I appreciated being able to spend each day with her.

"You're so funny!"

I heard Lily giggling from the kitchen.

I waited upstairs in the nursery for Lily to watch over Sadie while I took some time for myself in our spa in the East wing of the estate.

With Sadie now walking, if not supervised she would escape her room to play hide and seek which she played so well that we once had the whole house staff searching for her.

While, I loved living on the estate, the large rooms made it difficult to find my live-in nanny who spent most of the time catering to Sasha.

I adored being with Sadie, but I sometimes needed some space to tend to my self-care needs.

While holding Sadie in my arms, I followed Lily's laugh into the kitchen.

She was leaning on the marble countertop next to the sink while Sasha playfully sprinkled water onto her cheek with his large fingers.

Her smooth, pale youthful skin illuminated as she stared up at him with her rosy cheeks beaming from her wide smile. Her blouse was unbuttoned down enough to reveal her large cleavage, which Sasha glanced at a few times, then meeting Lily's eyes with a knowing look.

"Lily, it's after 10 in the morning you were supposed to be in the nursery at 9:45."

"Oh, sorry!" Lily brushed her platinum blonde hair behind her ears.

Sasha didn't turn around from the sink, he just continued pretending to rinse his coffee cup.

"Um, did you want some breakfast? Sasha just made some pancakes."

"No, just take Sadie upstairs please."

Lily reluctantly walked towards me and reached out to gather Sadie into her arms.

Sadie refused at first, holding onto the strap of my sports bra.

Sadie could not decide if she liked Lily or not. One day she was happy to see her, the next she would cry loudly when she came near.

Luckily, Sadie relaxed into Lily's arms as she left the kitchen.

I turned to exit the kitchen behind Lily.

"Are you going to have some breakfast?" Sasha finally turned around looking up with his large dark brown eyes.

"No. I'm on a diet."

I rushed out of the kitchen trying to hold back my humiliation and rage. I knew something more was happening between them, though I have not caught them in the act, my gut told me something was up.

I often tried to avoid Sasha.

I even went as far as to sleep in a separate room using

the excuse of me feeling discomfort after having Sadie.

After almost a year, I'm sure Sasha knew I was lying but decided not to push it.

The first month this was true as my body went through some uncomfortable changes after giving birth.

I rolled my eyes every time I recalled how obsessed I was with him before marrying him.

I made my way down the long wooden paneled hall to the large double doors leading to the spa area.

I had to admit, being married to Sasha came with some great perks. I complained about him a lot, but I lived like a queen with my own fully equipped gym, sauna, hair and makeup salon, outdoor pool, and indoor lap pool. I rarely had to leave the house for anything. He even let me turn one of the bedrooms into a massive closet to house all of the designer clothing that was sent to me.

I also never had to clean or maintain the estate, there was a team of staff that did everything.

When I reminded myself of this, I always came to the realization that maybe turning a blind eye to his faults was not so bad after all.

I removed my clothes and settled on the wooded bench in the sauna and let the cares of Lily and Sasha fade away.

"You need to fire that nanny." Jani lounged on an inflatable pool float next to me in the outdoor pool sipping a margarita.

She often came over to lounge by the pool. Every time, she made a point to tell me to fire the nanny.

"Oh, Jani, not this again."

"I'm serious! The last thing you need is some nubile, busty blonde hanging around the house all the time. These women want to live our lives so bad, and will do anything to get it. That's why they apply for these positions in wealthy neighborhoods."

She was right.

After marrying Sasha, I had encountered many women who would do anything to get to him, even Jani had tried on several occasions. And, I guess having Lily around lowered her chances to snag him for herself.

I was cautious with Jani and did not trust her, but with the circle of wives being so small, I had no better alternatives for friends.

I floated next to her and contemplated her advice to fire Lily.

"Trust me, Sam. You need to get rid of her as soon as possible."

Jani took another sip of her margarita.

"Everyone knows when hiring a nanny never chose a young woman. You might as well pack your bags and hand her the keys to the estate because your husband will sleep with her. Guaranteed."

It seemed she was speaking from experience. Everyone knew that her and Laney, the lead guitarist for Derelict's Rising, were having issues in their marriage.

I remember reading an article in a gossip magazine years ago about him cheating on Jani with their nanny, who was in her 20's and beautiful.

Whenever the band had an appearance they were rarely seen together. And, she spent most of her time here at their county home in Sussex instead of with him at their flat in London.

With Sasha and I having an estate of over 20,000 square feet on 70 acres of land, I could tell she wished she had ended up with Sasha instead.

He made a lot more money than the other band members with endorsement deals and appearances. He even had an investment portfolio and properties worth over 500 million dollars.

The other band members were so envious they rarely came around or even spoke to Sasha at public events.

I looked past Jani out over the beautifully landscaped gardens and lush forest that surrounded the property and suddenly felt that I could possibly lose it all.

I could not get Jani's warning about Lily taking my place out of my mind.

After she left, it troubled me the rest of the day.

I laid in bed for hours thinking about how easy it would be to lose everything to Lily. Sasha fell in love so easily, he would likely impregnate her the same as with me and move her right in.

He always loved a damsel in distress.

The thought reminded me of the night he needed to rescue Lexi when her and Sha argued at our engagement party in Malibu.

I needed to get rid of Lily, but this was not the best time to fire her because soon Sasha's son would be living with us full-time and the thought of raising two small children without any assistance troubled me.

After seeing how Sasha's lawyers discredited and humiliated the mother of his son in the courts for almost a year and took full custody made me fearful of the same happening to me.

I should start being more affectionate with Sasha. We had not made love in months.

But now, I needed to save my marriage.

It was 10 minutes past midnight and I decided now was as good a time as any to seduce him.

I slid out of bed and pulled a long, pink silk rode over my nude body. I quietly opened my door to not wake Sadie in the adorning room.

I made my way to Sasha's room and opened the heavy wooden door. The room was dark and his bed was made. I realized he had not been to his room all night.

I could feel the blood rush to my face as my breath quickened.

Immediately, I ran down the grand staircase to the foyer and through the staff quarters where the housekeeper and Lily slept.

I opened Lily's bedroom door and just as Sasha's room, her bed was made.

My heart pounded so that I could feel its vibration building pressure in my ears.

I automatically ran down the hall and my stomach dropped when I saw the light from under Sasha's office door.

As I moved closer my legs became heavy as if to stop me from discovering what I already knew.

I heard movements and whispers from his office and couldn't ignore the obvious any longer.

With the last of my strength, I pushed the heavy door open and in the glow of the wrought iron chandelier Lily's iridescent naked body was straddling Sasha in his large leather chair.

Sweat glistened from Sasha's dark hairy chest as they both froze in place and stared back at me.

I melted to the floor as my throat closed with my tongue thickening, blocking me from uttering a word.

Sasha pushed Lily on top of the desk and ran towards me with his large manhood hanging between his thick muscular thighs swinging limply.

He bent down and wrapped his arms around me. The soft wet hair on his chest engulfed my face making it even more difficult for me to breathe.

He lifted my face up to his, then kissed me deeply.

I started to pull away but he held me tightly and began peeling my sweat drenched robe from my skin.

He pulled me to my feet and guided me towards Lily who was still sitting on top of the desk.

I stood stiffly between her thighs as Sasha pressed his erection against my behind.

The warmth radiating from both their bodies excited me and I began to relax as Lily stroked my hair and leaned in pressing her lips against mine.

I could taste Sasha on her tongue as she slid it delicately into my mouth.

I cupped my hand over her smooth supple breast and climbed onto the desk next to her. She pushed me onto my back then spread my legs open while rubbing her hands over my sex.

My nerves took over and my body began shivering slightly from the stimulation of her fingertips gently stroking me.

She lowered her mouth onto the pink flesh gently running the tastebuds of her small tongue and flicking it at the end. Shivers moved down my spine each time she did this.

As ecstasy tingled over my skin, Sasha's muscular body glistened in the dimmed lights as he loomed over us with his piercing dark eyes staring wildly into mine. He stroked himself, then grabbed the back of my head and put himself into my mouth.

I could barely open my mouth wide enough to take in all of him.

On the verge of orgasm he frantically grabbed Lily by her hair and pulled her to the floor, then grabbed my leg and spun me towards him.

Without hesitation he shoved himself inside me and

pounded so hard the smacking of his pelvis against my skin echoed loudly in the room.

He threw his head back and his deep voice boomed in ecstasy as his warmth filled me.

All I could do was stare up at him.

"I love you." These were the last words I expected to escape his lips.

I looked towards the floor at Lily and she stared back at me baffled by Sasha's confession as well.

"Don't worry about her. She means nothing to me."

"What?" Lily jumped up from the floor.

Her luminous skin was now bright red as she ran up behind Sasha.

"NOTHING! You said you could not live without me!"

"My wife is here. It's time for you to go to your room." Sasha pointed at the door with his back sternly positioned at her.

Sasha lifted me from the desk and pointed towards the door again this time turning his head to look at her.

"I'm not going anywhere! You promised me we would be together!"

"No, I did not. I made it very clear what this was." Sasha's voice grew angry.

"You lying piece of SHIT! You will not get away with this! I'm telling everyone what a lying snake you are!"

Lily began grabbing the leather bound books from the shelves facing Sasha's desk and throwing them in our direction. Her aim was off but one managed to hit him on his head.

He nearly dropped me, but I caught my balance as my feet hit the floor. He ran around me and lifted Lily from the ground pinning her arms.

She struggled in his grasp and kicked her legs wildly as he carried her out of the office.

He shoved her into the hallway, then quickly ran back into the office and closed the door.

Lily pounded on the door in rage as he struggled to lock it.

The whole time I just stood behind the desk watching helplessly.

Sasha now stiff and breathing heavy from overexertion made his way to the landline phone.

"Get this crazy bitch out of my house!"

He slammed the phone down and within minutes the pounding stopped and all I could hear was Lily's muffled cries as Sasha's personal security guard carried her away.

3

"We've gone platinum!"

Sasha shouted over the crowd backstage as he sprayed champagne on everyone in the room. The photographers' cameras flashed continuously as they frantically moved around hoping to get the best shots for the blogs and magazines.

The band's greatest hits album was certified platinum.

They received the news a few days before their performance in the "Youth and Music" charity concert in London to support musical education in grade schools.

I looked around the room for Jani, she would never miss a moment to be photographed with the band.

With the room filled with promoters, executives, and younger women, I looked forward to her company since there was no one else to talk to.

Everyone always just stared at me as if I was the thing that should not be touched.

A young brunette with plump red cheeks handed each of the band members a large framed plaque with a platinum record engraved with the band's name.

Sasha was so proud. The past few months he tried to hide his fear of being irrelevant in the music industry, so I knew how much this meant to him. I teared up with joy because I knew how hard he worked and I got to share this moment with him.

I was quickly brought back to reality when one of the photographers camera's flashed in my face. My eyes strained to focus as the photographer started asking me questions about our daughter.

Luckily, Renae scolded him. She made him delete the unflattering photos and retake them with me posing in my designer outfit that was sent to me for this occasion.

The public relations for the band's record label wanted to preserve Sasha's imagine as a womanizing bad boy, so our family life was not often publicized unless the media discussed how Sasha took me from a younger rock star, Fred.

I tried to make my way to him so that I could congratulate him, but everyone surrounded him begging for his attention.

I laid my hand on his arm, but he didn't notice it was me and pulled away when his manager called him out of the room to take pictures with fans who paid for meet and greets.

I walked to the catering table and picked up a bottle of water hoping no one noticed.

"You excited about the band's platinum album?"

One of the lower level executives tried to make small talk. His kind eyes showed his lack of experience in this cut throat industry, but his naivety would not last long.

"I am. Sasha worked so hard in the studio."

"So, how's your daughter?"

"She's great and back home with our new nanny. I miss her so much. I can't wait until she's old enough to bring to the shows."

"Well, with your beauty and Sasha's talent, she's going to grow up to be great."

"Thank you."

The executive smiled sweetly and left the room with a group of stage hands. He was the only one who seemed to empathize with the difficulties I encountered being the wife of Sasha.

I appreciated his kindness, but I would feel better if Jani was here.

A stage hand escorted me and the other band members' guests and wives to a seating area in the stands designated for us. I sat at the front row and everyone else sat with the people they came with. Only a few of the guests intermingled, but as usual everyone stayed with their own group and no one sat next to me.

I watched Sasha's personal bodyguard as he escorted about ten young women in their early 20's to the side of the stage. They all dressed provocatively in black mini skirts or tight pants with their assets on full display.

The excitement on their faces brought on a nostalgic feeling of when I was like them having an experience of a lifetime.

I watched them knowing that this would be the most exciting thing to ever happen to them.

While I was envious of their youthful wonder for life, I wouldn't go back to being just another faceless groupie in a crowd begging to be chosen just for one night.

Breaking News! Derelict's Rising guitarist Laney and former supermodel Jani have filed for divorce!

I was shocked seeing the headline on the front page of the newspaper.

Jani always loved being in the press, but I'm sure

reading 'former' supermodel was not sitting well with her.

Now, I understand why she wasn't at the show last night.

I sat at a small table by the window of our hotel suite looking over Kensington Gardens.

Sasha left earlier this morning for meetings. I found it odd he got a hotel suite for us when I knew he kept a house somewhere in London.

I asked for the newspaper to be delivered with my breakfast because I thought me and Sasha would be on the front, but I did not expect to see Jani's demise plastered on the front page.

I was a little elated when I saw the headline because Jani always projected herself as the head rock star wife. With all the unsolicited advice she gave to the rest of us, it seemed she should have been taking it herself.

I thought it would take more effort to take her position, but her now ex-husband gave me a head start.

I frantically combed though the pages to read the full story of what happened. In the center of the article's page there was a picture of Laney with a woman in her early twenties. I recognized her as one of the girls standing side stage at the show last night. She was hard to miss as she stood by the stage as though it belonged to her.

I'll never forget the tattooed sleeve covering her left arm. She was very petit with straight dark red hair past her waist. She was the total opposite of Jani's American beach blond aesthetic.

While I found this amusing, I was also sad because Jani was the only wife in the band who acknowledged me.

Although her motives were selfish, I still enjoyed having someone who understood this lifestyle to talk with. The other wives still saw me as a threat since many of them were now pushing 50 years and their husbands might get inspired to trade them in for a younger wife.

With her and Laney divorcing, the older wives I'm sure are more worried now. I was also a little concerned since his new girlfriend was even younger than me.

The wives would eventually shun Jani since she would not be allowed to any of the bands' events. And, she would be a reminder of what could happen to them.

It was so sad that she was now an outcast in a world she once dominated.

Derelict's Rising agreed to perform an additional night for the "Youth and Music" charity since the first concert sold out so quickly.

This time only the wives were allowed backstage. After the news of Laney and Jani, no groupies were allowed at the concert.

The other wives were suddenly eager to have me join them for drinks at the bar backstage before the show.

I guess with Jani's divorce and younger replacement, the ladies needed the three of us to stay close to block any other newcomers from knocking another one of us off our throne.

Luckily for me, Sasha wasn't married when I met him, so this gave me a pass to finally join the club, now that they were down one member.

"I'm glad you decided to join us, Sam." Caitlin, the drummer's wife, flipped her shoulder length dark hair and stared down at me with her small dark brown eyes. She always tilted her head upward in an aristocratic way when she spoke. Of all the wives she was the oldest at 49 and never had any plastic surgery, choosing to age gracefully.

"Well, thank you for inviting me." I took a sip of my red

wine blend which was all the small backstage bar had to offer that wasn't hard liquor.

"So, have you heard from Jani? We know you two were close." Fifi, the bassist's wife, was from Normandy, France and always spoke in almost a whisper with her face expressionless from the years of facial procedures. She was very slim with long dirty blond hair that was always slightly unkempt.

"I haven't spoken to her since the news broke. I texted her but she never responded."

Caitlin and Fifi gave each other a worried look.

"It's really unfortunate what's happening to her. I wonder what she will do now?" Fifi's eyes showed a slight sadness.

As the three of us sat in our mourning of Jani's divorce my phone chimed.

It was Jani.

Jani: Hey, I'm outside by the back entrance. Can you come out here? Security won't let me in.

"It's Jani. She says security won't let her in."

I stood from the table and made my way down the hall to the back entrance with Caitlin and Fifi following close behind.

I saw Jani and Laney's two teenage sons standing outside in front of the security guard whose hands were raised in protest to Jani yelling at him to step aside.

"Excuse me! I am coming in with my son's."

Jani saw me approaching the door.

"Sam! Tell him I am supposed to be back here!"

I stepped out the back door, but Caitlin and Fifi stayed inside.

"Hey! How are you?" I wrapped my arms around Jani

but she didn't return my embrace.

"I can't let her pass." The guard blocked the doorway shaking his head.

Tears welled in the corners of Jani's eyes as she realized she no longer had access to this world.

"Hey, after the show come by the hotel and we'll have a drink. Okay?"

"I can't believe he's doing this to me." Her voice was strained as she tried to hold back her tears.

A few onlookers held up their cellphones recording Jani.

"We'll meet later, okay?"

Jani's expression changed to anger as she stared into my eyes.

"No, I'm fine. But, maybe you should visit your husband's second home here in London?"

She turned away with her shoulders hunched over leaving me standing frozen in confusion.

The guard escorted the two boys down the hall to Laney's dressing room.

I finally turned around to see Caitlin and Fifi huddled together staring at me.

"Poor thing. That was so humiliating." Caitlin shook her head in disbelief.

"I guess we won't be seeing her around anymore." Fifi said sadly.

Another security guard came to manage the door and the three of us made our way back to the small bar to finish our wine and gossip in disbelief of what we witnessed.

Part II: Lexi

4

"Is breakfast almost ready! I'm starving in here!"

Sasha's voice boomed from his office as I hurried around the kitchen multitasking flipping the pancakes and making the coffee.

I knew he had the benefit concert last night, but was not fully expecting him to show up here since Sam was in London as well.

I should have known better and had the house in order sooner.

Before, he used to call in advance so that I could prepare. But, lately he has started showing up unannounced.

Most times he was in his office organizing contracts and having conference calls. He worked a lot and always had several projects going at the same time.

I admired this about him, but often times I spent these visits catering to him.

"Will I be able to eat my breakfast before my phone call?"

He stood in the kitchen entryway staring annoyed at

my attempts.

"It's ready. I just need to set everything out."

"Well, let's get it on the table. You knew I was in town, why did you not start cooking earlier?"

I rolled my eyes clearly ignoring his question and continued plating the food.

He was so demanding that I actually started to enjoy the times he was not here, giving me the freedom and peace to do what I wanted. But, I knew not to get too upset with him because as my mother always reminded me, he pays for everything.

Sasha's conference calls would take a few hours so I decided to quickly thaw a small roast in some ice water to slow cook in the crockpot to give me some time to clean the upstairs.

After cleaning the bathroom and clearing the clothes from the floor, I made my way downstairs to prepare lunch since the roast would not be done for another two hours.

I could hear Sasha talking but with the door closed making everything sound mumbled. But, when I heard a series of sure, uh hums, and sighs, I knew he had given his demands and was ready to end the last call.

I did not have much in the refrigerator, so I sliced a few pieces of half eaten cheese with some salami. Thankfully, I had some baguettes in the freezer to quickly bake.

I rushed to have everything laid out on the coffee table in the living room before Sasha ended his call because I did not want a repeat of his complaining from this morning.

I opened a bottle of Provence rose wine and with perfect timing poured a glass for Sasha just as he exited from his office.

He kissed my cheek, pleased with the food on the table.

"Thank you. But, do we have some Champagne? I would prefer that for lunch."

Sasha's phone vibrated on the coffee table next to the half eaten slices of roast and stewed vegetables we picked over for dinner.

"Stay quiet, it's Sam."

He went to the toilet closet to take the call.

I pulled the throw blanket around my nude body as I made my way into the kitchen to open another bottle of Bordeaux.

It still made me uncomfortable when Sam called while he was here.

I heard the toilet flush and waited in the kitchen for Sasha to end his call and exit the toilet before coming back into the living room.

It was after 6 o'clock and the sun was setting. I knew he couldn't stay the night.

It's funny how I got annoyed when he just popped over, but felt sad when he had to leave.

I carried the bottle of wine into the living room and he stood there naked looking down at his phone. I loved seeing his muscles from behind tighten with every slight move he made.

His dark black hair was longer than usual hanging just past the nape of his neck.

"I opened another bottle."

Startled, he turned around and stared directly into my eyes.

He quickly sat his phone on the side table furthest from me and his eyes became gentle and loving again.

He grabbed the bottle from my grasp and poured us both a glass.

"I have to leave in a little while."

"I know."

We both settled onto the couch and he pulled the throw over both our laps.

"So, what have you been up to when I'm away."

He normally didn't ask about my time alone. It seemed he was trying to make small talk to avoid the awkwardness of his wife calling.

"Well, I've been writing more."

"Really, what have you been writing?"

I sat up to face him.

"I want to try writing for other musicians. I need a new agent because the one you introduced me to in Los Angeles has not been doing anything nor returning my calls. I am ready to expand and create my own brand in the industry." For a while I've wanted to discuss with him my desire to work with other artists, but was to afraid of offending him.

Sasha grimaced and cleared his throat.

"Who exactly do you want to write for?"

"Well, I don't know specifically, but I know that I want to expand my portfolio to include more musicians."

He looked down into his wine glass.

"Sasha, I love writing for you but you only used one of the songs I wrote on the new album."

He turned to face me.

"Lexi, these things take time. You should understand that by now."

"I do understand. It's just I have so many ideas and I want to really push myself to do more with my writing."

"Am I not doing enough for you?" His voice raised slightly and the expression on his face became tense.

My throat tightened.

"You do so much for me. You know I am happy working

with you. I just feel that I have so much potential to really expand my reach with musicians in other genres. I just want a chance to do more."

The room became silent as I waited for what felt like forever for Sasha to respond.

"I'll look into it, but you remember what happened when you wrote for Sha and I had to help you. I am protecting you Lexi. This business is full of sharks and I have done everything to ensure you never have to go through that again."

He pulled the throw from his lap and stood up.

"I should get going. Um, give me about two weeks to find something for you."

"Okay."

I sat quietly as he picked up his clothes from the arm chair and began dressing himself.

The room was tense and I felt I'd made a huge mistake. It almost felt as if his leaving was a punishment.

After he finished dressing he stood over me, then raised my chin in his large hand and looked deeply into my eyes.

"I hear you Lexi and I agree that you should work with other artists. I will find someone trustworthy to help you, okay."

"Okay."

He lean forward and kissed me.

"I love you."

"I love you, too."

5

"You need to be more careful, Lexi." My mom scolded me over the phone after I told her about asking Sasha to let me write for other musicians.

"He takes very good care of you. What you need to focus on is getting him to leave that backstabber of a so-called friend of yours and marry you."

"Mom! Really!"

"Yes, really." She snapped back.

After my mom came to visit me in London, she was very impressed with how well I was living here. Now, all she talks about is how I should be pursuing Sasha and taking him from Sam.

The thought of living under his thumb and not having the freedom and space to do my own thing made me shiver.

"Ma, I care about Sasha. I really do. But, I have dreams and goals that I want to attain."

"Well, it sounds like those dreams and goals are gonna get you kicked out and alone."

"Come on, Ma."

"I thought I taught my daughter better than that. You can have both, but you need to focus on keeping that good man you got."

"Mom, you are so old-school. Women don't need marry a man to secure their future these days."

"Oh! And, here you are telling me this from the comfort of the home a man pays for you to stay in. Not just any home, but a multi-million dollar home in posh London. You have no idea how blessed you are. Men these days don't do things like that."

"I hear you mom."

"I'm just looking out for my daughter, that's all."

It seemed everyone was looking out for me to the point of not allowing me to make my own decisions.

"I know mom. I just called to share the good news that I may be able to work with other musicians and really get my name out there."

My mother sighed loudly.

"I guess congratulations, Lexi. I hope this works out for you. And, if it doesn't you can always come home."

"Thanks for the confidence, mom."

"You know what, I have to go. Call me when you get some sense, Lexi."

I was relieved when the call disconnected.

It was lonely being here in London and my mom was the only person I could talk to about Sasha.

My neighbors avoided me since they knew Sasha and I were sneaking around together. And, the people who pursued a friendship with me were just trying to use me to get into the industry.

When I wasn't being a hermit, the only other thing that soothed me was shopping.

And, Sasha was very generous.

I saved some of the money he sent me, but not enough

with all the retail therapy nearby.

I still had the jewelry Sha bought me and I never spent the fifty thousand dollars that I saved in Los Angeles. With that and not having to pay any bills, I've been able to save up over a hundred thousand dollars.

But, I knew that was not enough to live on if Sasha ever decided to leave me for good.

The thought scared me as I had grown accustomed to this lifestyle.

But, the loneliness was getting to me.

*

"We also have this one in blue."

The salesperson sat the small leather purse on the counter. It was from the new collection.

"There were only a few of these made. It is very exclusive."

I always spent a ton of money in this upscale department store and the salespeople literally chased me down with so-called exclusive items for me to purchase.

This time it was the tall thin pale man in his thirties, who always wore a silk scarf around his neck.

He has sold a lot of things to me in the past and was very persistent.

It was a beautiful purse and I realized did not have that color in my collection.

I handed over my credit card and he swiftly swiped it at the register. The purse was wrapped, boxed, and bagged quickly before I could change my mind.

Somehow he was also able to convince me to try on some dresses to match my new purse.

It made no sense why I bought these things since other than my date nights with Sasha, I didn't have many places to wear my new luxuries.

After spending more than I wanted to, I decided to get some takeout for dinner and get back home before another salesperson hunted me down.

Luckily, I was able to make it out of the store and into a black cab with no one stopping me.

The euphoric feeling from my purchases never lasted long. I always realized that I did not need any more stuff to just sit in the back of my closet.

The black cab pulled onto my street and just ahead I spotted a woman trying to peer into my window.

"Can you drop me off here?"

The cab stopped a few doors down from my place.

I paid my fare and cautiously stepped out of the cab.

The woman walked down the stairs from my door and stood on the sidewalk with her back to me.

As I slowly approached her, she suddenly turned around as if sensing my presence.

It was Sam.

I was surprised that I did not recognize her at first. She seemed so different now.

We both froze in place, standing only a few feet away from each other.

Pain flashed across her face as she stood there staring back at me.

I couldn't utter a word.

Then, she turned away and walked quickly down the street.

6

I sat at the kitchen table quietly picking at my scrambled eggs.

After seeing Sam, I barely slept at all. I just tossed and turned all night.

And, I wasn't sure if I even felt guilty.

I just felt weird.

I waited by the phone for Sasha to call about Sam knowing I was living here. Then, I realized he could ask me to leave and decide never to see me again.

I could see Sam demanding Sasha to get rid of me.

And, with her being the wife and mother of his child, it was likely for him to appease her demands.

How did I let my whole life get wrapped up in Sasha?

My chest began to ache at the thought of not being able to write and losing out on my chance to have a solid career in the music industry.

Now, I began regretting all those frivolously expensive shopping sprees I went on. Why did I not save that money?

Who was I kidding? Even if I had more money saved,

one bad word from Sasha and my dreams were over.

Realizing my life could be over in a matter of minutes, I needed to make a plan for the worse.

I took a deep breath and made my way up the stairs to my bedroom. I didn't bother making the bed or picking the clothes up from the floor. What was the point?

I still had my books with the middle cut out when I hid my jewelry from Johnny back in Los Angeles. I kept them hidden in a plan black duffle bag. Since Sasha flew me to London on his private plane, I didn't have to worry about sneaking them in unnoticed.

Well, I had enough money saved to rent a small apartment for a year, then I could take my time pawning each piece of jewelry.

If I'm lucky, I could also take the clothes and purses with me. I would definitely pawn those since I barely wore any of them.

Oddly, I began feeling calmer as I organized my possessions.

My phone chimed with an incoming text message.

Suddenly, the air became heavy and my chest caved in when I saw the text notification was from Sasha.

I took another deep breath and opened the message.

Sasha: I thought about what you said and you are right. You are talented and should be working with more artists. I spoke to an agent I know personally. I will introduce you to her one day soon. I will be out of the country for a few weeks. We'll do something fun when I get back. Love, S.

I reread the text message.

He didn't mention Sam being here last night.

I wondered if she told him?

Could she be waiting for the right moment to bring it up?

Did he know and just did not care that Sam knew about me being here?

More questions rattled my mind.

I didn't know whether to be excited about Sasha helping me or worried that he or Sam was not saying anything.

I sat on the bed staring into my black duffle bag of books filled with my jewelry.

I decided to keep my jewelry hidden in these books just in case. From my experience anything can happen.

I reorganized my clothes back into the walk-in closet and hide my duffle bag where Sasha couldn't find it.

My cellphone chimed again.

I froze in the middle of the closet.

Was it Sasha again?

I grabbed my phone from the bed and was shocked to see a direct message notification from Johnny on my social media account.

Sitting on the edge of the bed, I hesitated opening the message.

I was finally calming down from the anticipation of Sasha's message, I really did not need anymore surprises right now.

I opened the message.

Johnny: Hey, I was thinking about you and saw you were living in London. The band will be doing a few shows out there in about a month and I would like to see you. Hope all is well.

I studied Johnny's profile picture with his dark black hair styled just below his ears. It was good he grew his hair back long, I never cared for it short.

I went through his feed and saw that he was posting more often and looked happy with travel photos with the band members 'Death of Love'. It seemed they were back together and recording a new album.

This was a shock because I had not heard anything about them touring.

I went back to his message and decided to reply.

Lexi: That's cool you guys are back together and touring. I'd love to see you perform.

He read the message immediately and I saw that he was replying.

Johnny: Cool. I'll put you on the list. You look good. See you.

I sat the phone on the bed.

After everything we went through together, I oddly did not experience any emotion from his message. Being away from him for so long, I eventually stopped thinking about him.

I wondered if I ever really loved him or was it his position in the band.

Now, I was wondering if I had any real feelings for Sasha.

Why was I here in this house alone most of the time, with no friends, no social outings, no connections with the outside world other than my mother?

I always just waited here for Sasha to show up.

And, when he did, we rarely went out anywhere with the fear that he would be recognized and pictures taken of us together.

I suddenly began feeling claustrophobic in this house.

All this time I was fooling myself thinking I was living a grand life when I really was not living at all.

Part III: Sam

7

"We should definitely do injections in the forehead area and between the brows."

The dermatologist ran his gloved hand across sections of my face as he examined my skin under a bright ring light.

"A few microdermabrasion procedures will address the fine lines in the outer corners of the eyes. And, I would do some fillers along the cheeks for a lifting effect."

A young female assistant listed all of his suggestions on a notepad, nodding each time.

After seeing Lexi at Sasha's London home, I could not get the thought of her being with him all this time out of my mind.

I always knew something likely happened between them, I just didn't know how serious it was.

I quickly regretted making this dermatology appointment. I felt worse about myself as the dermatologist pointed out all of the imperfections on my face.

This was our last day in London before going on

holiday to Sardinia, Italy.

I wanted to avoid Sasha until our daughter and his children showed up at the hotel. I could not be alone with him without wanting to burst into tears.

"Okay."

The dermatologist adjusted my bed so that I was sitting upright and facing him.

He was likely in his 50's but his face was so smooth and plump he looked a lot younger. But, every time his spoke it set frozen with only his eyes and lips moving. This made it difficult for me to pay attention because I was trying not to offend him by staring.

"Here are my suggestions for your treatment."

He handed me a sheet of paper with a face diagram and notes on the areas he wanted to do procedures.

"I'm going to give you a prescription for a retinoid cream. Start out using it twice a week and once you get used to it move to three times a week. And, wear a higher spf sunscreen because this will make you burn easily in the sun."

He stared blankly into my eyes.

"Do you have any questions?"

"No, I will look everything over." I spoke almost in a whisper.

"Okay, Lacy will walk you out and I look forward to seeing you after your vacation."

I could not get out of that office fast enough.

He came highly recommended by Jani a few months ago. She said he worked on all the English celebrities.

Now in my thirties, I wanted to look my best and keep my youthfulness, but I was not sure this was the best option.

I had two hours left before Sasha's children would show up, so I stopped at a small cafe a block from the dermatologist's office.

I ordered a latte and decided against a pastry now that my nutritionist has me on a low carb diet. I settled at a corner table by the large window and slowly sipped my latte.

At a table just outside the window sat a young couple embracing each other. They looked so at ease and pleased with life as they enjoyed the late Spring weather.

Suddenly, I felt something was missing.

I recalled how Fred and I would sit at the cafe near his apartment like this. Everything was so easy and free.

After New York, he disappeared from the music scene and the band broke up.

I never went back to Paris to get my belongings.

Now, that I had new, more expensive clothes and jewelry, I didn't feel any pressure to get my things back.

I remembered how sweet the love making was between Fred and I. It was also once that way with Sasha, but now it felt more like an obligation to keep him satisfied.

Sasha needed a lot of sex.

Every night we were together, he just pounced on me. Sometimes several times in one night. I could not keep up with his sexual needs.

My cellphone vibrated in my purse.

Assuming it was Sasha demanding I return to the hotel, I was slow to answer.

To my surprise it was a direct message from Craig on my social media profile.

Craig: I told you the band was getting back together. We'll be playing in London soon. Come out and see us. I'd love to catch up.

I stared at the message and before I could respond Sasha

called.

"Are you on your way back? The kids are here and we're heading out for dinner."

"Okay, I'm on my way back now."

"We'll meet you in the lobby."

I decided not to respond to Craig's message. This was my life now and I already had to deal with Lexi.

Sneaking around with Craig would only justify Sasha's cheating.

I was not ready to give up on my marriage and the lifestyle it afforded me just yet.

Sorry, Craig.

8

"Ahhhh!"

Sadie was throwing a legendary temper tantrum in the restaurant.

Laney and his new girlfriend, Casey, glanced in annoyance at me as I handed Sadie kicking and screaming to Dijon, our new nanny, or manny as he preferred to be called.

I felt safer with Dijon because not only was he not going to seduce Sasha, his large muscular body ensured Sadie would be protected in his care.

Sasha was hesitant at first to hire him after being faced with a very handsome, fit 32-year-old with smooth dark skin and a posh London accent.

But, with his 4-year-old son, Sean, moving in with us, we needed a good live-in nanny immediately. And, he had stellar references.

Dijon quickly handed Sadie a small, plush doll that played music every time she squeezed it. This kept her attention for the rest of the dinner.

Sean, unlike Sadie, was very quiet and polite. He sat

next to Dijon and watched Sadie in her highchair playing with her musical doll.

"It's time for the kids to go to bed." Sasha, like everyone at the table, was now annoyed by the doll's repeated song with Sadie squealing.

Dijon, barely having time to touch his food, swiftly picked up Sadie and held Sean's hand then the three of them quickly headed towards the hotel's elevators.

The waiter came over to collect Dijon's untouched plate.

I was under the impression this would be an intimate family dinner, but his two older children decided to go out into the city center for dinner instead. And, Laney invited himself to dinner since he lived close by.

Laney followed Sasha around like a puppy dog.

Sasha was always the star in the room and Laney could only hope that some of his stardust would land on him.

Now that it was just the four of us, I could pay more attention to Casey.

As Sasha and Laney talked about the upcoming tour, she put on a full performance.

Holding her body upright and displaying a stoic expression. She expertly handled sitting with rock royalty with aplomb.

She wore an asymmetrical black dress that only exposed her left arm with a full sleeve tattoo of a red dragon slaying an army of men. Her make-up was caked on heavily with black winged eyeliner and red lipstick. This was something only a younger woman with smooth skin could pull off.

Every time she sipped her red wine, she'd cock her head back confidently and took the slowest sip.

Occasionally, she made eye contact with Sasha, but looked away before seeming too obvious.

"So, what do you do, Casey?" Sasha turned to focus his

45

attention on her making Laney slightly jealous.

"I'm an influencer on social media." She batted her eyes seductively at Sasha.

"Really?" Sasha said with a smirk. "Are you actually earning money, or do you work for likes and attention?"

Like many English people from my experience Sasha had no filter with his words.

Casey looked over to Laney expecting him to defend her, but he avoided her glance with no intention of helping her.

"I earn my own money and I work very hard at my craft." Her body stiffened.

"Craft! You mean taking provocative photos and posting them for some old man to spend his money on you." Sasha started laughing loudly.

"She actually gets sponsor deals to promote their products." Laney finally decided to grow a backbone.

"Audience! Who is your audience?" Sasha struggled to speak from laughing so hard.

"I have over a million followers. And, I am currently negotiating with three brands who are willing to pay me thousands of pounds to promote their products." She pouted her lips at Sasha and rolled her eyes.

"Oh! So, you're selling poo poo tea and cheap clothes." Sasha's voice carried throughout the restaurant and other diners began staring at us.

"At least I make my own money and don't need to live off of another man." She glanced in my direction with a snarl.

The table became quiet.

I turned my attention back to my plate and sat in silence finishing my meal as Sasha and Laney went back to discussing the upcoming tour.

* * *

"That man definitely has a type. Airheads who think they're so smart and won't shut up!"

Sasha laid back on the bed wearing his reading glasses and reviewing marketing plans for his scotch brand.

I sat on a chaise lounge at the foot of the bed sorting his clothes in his suitcase.

"I remember when he was first dating Jani. That woman would never shut up. She thought because she was a supermodel everyone wanted to hear her opinion on everything. And, this little tart, who's obviously using poor dumb Laney, is just a younger version of her."

"She seems to make him happy." I said looking up from the suitcase.

"She is all he can get." Sasha glared at me and pulled his reading glasses on top of his head.

"What do you mean?" I stopped sorting his clothes.

He sat up ready to spill the gossip. One thing about Sasha, he loved to gossip.

"Well, Laney is not as financially secure as he wants people to think. That's the real reason he and Jani are divorcing."

"What?" I moved onto the bed and closer to him.

"He was never good with his money. Over the years, he made stupid investments with some shady people and spent more than he made. On a few occasions, I had to loan him money that he never paid back, of course."

He took a sip of his scotch. I leaned forward waiting for him to say more.

"Jani has been footing the bill for their whole lifestyle. He even persuaded her to cash out her annuity and they spent all of it. Now, that he is expecting to receive money from the upcoming tour and new album sales, he wants to divorce Jani before she can claim it in court."

"Oh, that's dirty!" My eyes widened.

"I know. But, this new tart he's dating will get the boot as soon as he gets his money and meets a woman with higher value."

"What do you mean, higher value?"

"The only reason he married Jani in the first place was because she was a famous supermodel. He was engaged to another woman he dated for years, then dumped her as soon as Jani showed interest in him. They both loved being in the magazines and at the fancy parties. That's why they don't have any money."

Sasha sat back and pulled his glasses back onto his face.

"And, as soon as he meets some famous woman to leach on, he will dump this new love interest." He picked up his marketing plans and went back to reading them.

"Wow. Poor girl."

"Oh, don't feel sorry for her. She's using him so she can get more social media followers to buy her poo poo tea."

9

I looked out the large windows of the yacht and watched the sail boats glide along the clear blue waters of Costa Smeralda in Sardinia, Italy.

Sasha rented a 200-foot yacht for the week.

At first I thought it was too much but with he and I, his three children, our daughter, the manny, his assistant, my assistant, two body guards, and the yacht crew, it was barely large enough for all of us.

This was my first time on a family trip with Sasha and his children. He planned a family trip to a different destination with them at least twice a year. And, with his hectic schedule, I found it heartwarming that he never failed to plan these trips with his children.

The captain was finally able to dock after 20 minutes of waiting.

The port was crowded with yachts and pedestrians walking along admiring the boats. After sailing in from the south of France, I could not wait to get to land and explore the town.

"The ship has docked! We can go into town now!"

Steven, Sasha's 13-year-old son jumped up and down on the deck.

He was the spitting image of Sasha with long dark hair and large deep, dark brown eyes.

"Will you stop jumping on the deck before you hurt yourself!" Sandy, Sasha's 30-year-old daughter from his first marriage scolded Steven as she often did when they were together.

Sandy looked nothing like Sasha with platinum blond hair cut just below her ears and bright green eyes. She was curvy and shorter than Steven at 5'2. I recalled watching the documentaries on Derelict's Rising and seeing the images of his first wife, Lacy. It was eerie how much Sandy resembled her mother. If her hair was longer she would look like her twin.

She was not as close to Sasha as the boys. I assumed it was because he identified with them more.

Sandy had an Ivy League university education and worked as a literary agent for many famous writers. With Sasha's connections she has been able to negotiate deals with the top publishing houses and film producers.

I thought with Sandy and I being so close in age that we would have a lot in common, but she often ignored me. When she did acknowledge me it was brief.

The few times she came to visit Sasha, she often seemed awkward and out of place. Her presence was more of a duty than a choice.

As we descended the stairs onto the port docks the heavily salty smell of the sea filled my nose.

I felt dizzy as I stood on the solid surface after swaying on the yacht for the past few hours.

We made our way up the hills and through the narrow streets.

I tried my best to ignore the onlookers crowding us

with their camera phones and pleas for autographs from Sasha.

Sandy and Steven seemed to enjoy the attention while Sean held on to my leg and buried his face into the skirt of my white dress. I was often worried about him since he barely spoke and refused to play with other children.

We followed Sasha to a quiet street he knew from his travels that was rarely busy. At the top of the hill that looked over the sea and town below there was an ice cream parlor. The older woman behind the counter was ecstatic to see Sasha and ran up to him to hug and kiss his cheeks.

They said a few words in Italian and Sasha pointed out each of us to her and she waved.

Sadie began crying while Dijon pushed her in the stroller behind me. My breast began to swell and I knew it was time for her feeding.

While everyone ran to the ice cream case to make their selection I cradled Sadie in my arms and found a quiet corner to feed her.

With her first birthday in a few months, I've been trying to wane her off of breastmilk and eating more solids, but she was very stubborn.

After the older woman handed everyone their ice cream, Sasha took an envelope from his personal security guard and placed it in the woman's hand. She refused at first but Sasha insisted. I suspected the envelope was full of money as the woman kissed his cheeks profusely.

Once Sadie was finished feeding she fell asleep so I placed her back in the stroller.

The old woman handed me an ice cream cone with a scoop of vanilla on top. She sat down and looked in on Sadie sleeping.

"Bella." She pointed at her.

"Thank you."

"Sasha, is good man." She said in her broken English while pointing at him.

All I could do was nod and smile as I tried to block the image of Lexi standing in front of his London home.

The next day we sailed to the island La Maddalena. This time we decided to have a family picnic on a pebbled beach in a semi private cove.

I sat on a white lounge chair and watched Sandy playing with Sadie and Sean in the pebbles. They seemed to enjoy themselves and I was pleased to see Sean laughing and running around. Steven was not too far away practicing the kicks he learned from his jiu jitsu class.

I looked around and saw Dijon taking a much needed break as he laid back on a towel sleeping.

There were a few people on the beach, but no one really paid attention to us as they swam in the water.

I finally started to relax when I saw a young woman with golden tanned skin in a yellow bikini talking to Sasha and his body guard. Her face was beaming as she flirted with him.

Sasha enjoyed the attention as he scanned his eyes over her body.

I tried to ignore this scene and pulled a book from my beach bag. As I read a few words, I got a strange feeling that something was not right.

Sandy obviously felt the same as I saw her staring worried in Sasha's direction.

I turned back and saw Sasha, his body guard, and the girl walking around a large rock into another cove and out of view.

Sandy made eye contact with me then looked away in

shame.

A knot grew in the pit of my belly as I knew what was happening.

I watched Sadie and Sean playing in the water and I became enraged that Sasha was behaving like this.

A crew member showed up to take everyone back to the yacht for lunch.

As Sandy and Dijon settled the children into the speed boat, I jumped up startling Sandy and marched toward the large rock.

As the boat sped away with everyone towards the yacht, I made my way around the large rock and spotted Sasha, the woman, and his bodyguard walking further down the cove, then wading through the water to go around into another private cove where no one could see them.

When I made my way around I was preparing to yell at Sasha but froze when I saw him.

He and his body guard were kneeling on a beach towel with the young woman on all fours sandwiched between them. She was performing with her mouth on Sasha while his body guard had her from behind.

Sasha's eyes were closed as his head tilted back and he let out a moan in ecstasy. I could not stop staring at him. He grasped to woman's hair in his hands and began pumping himself in and out of her mouth.

I could tell he was close to climaxing with his body tense and blood rushing to his face.

He looked up and caught me watching him.

I expected him to be shocked, but instead he stared into my eyes with a smirk and continued pushing himself rapidly in and out of the woman's mouth.

The remainder of the trip Sean and Sadie slept with me

while Sasha stayed in their room.

I could barely look at him let alone speak to him after the beach scene in La Maddalena.

We made our way to our final destination in Villefranche-sur-mer.

After docking the yacht at the port, Sasha, Steven, and his body guard went into town while Sandy and I went for a walk leaving Sean and Sadie sleeping onboard with Dijon.

After La Maddalena, Sandy has been going out of her way to be kind to me. I knew she felt pity for me in my unhappy marriage.

As we walked quietly along the port, I could tell she wanted to say something but was searching for the right moment.

"Why do you let him treat you this way?" She finally blurted out.

"What can I do?" I looked into her bright green eyes.

"You can leave him. I know you saw him with that woman on the beach." She searched my face for a reaction. "Is it the money? Is that why you put up with his crap?"

"We have a child together. I can't put her through a long, stressful divorce."

"But, you choose to put her through a long, stressful marriage."

I tried my best to stay calm, but frustration began building up inside of me.

"How can you put up with this? I would never let a man treat me like that." She rolled her eyes in judgement.

"You don't have to put up with any type of treatment because you are a spoiled brat who had your whole life handed to you on a silver plater. You don't know what it's like to struggle. So, don't preach to me about my marriage!"

I turned around and stormed off toward the yacht.

Who does that product of nepotism think she is scolding me about my marriage?

But, deep down I knew she was right.

If Sasha was not an iconic wealthy rock star, I would not put up with any of his shenanigans.

Although at the beginning, I did love him. I knew I wanted this lifestyle. I fought for this and I was not going back to being that poor girl living in South Georgia.

Our last night on the yacht in Villefrance-sur-mer was quiet. I decided to eat in my room alone while everyone else went into town for dinner.

The next day, Sasha sent the children with Dijon on a private plane back to London while he and I chartered another private plane to Paris.

He planned for us to spend a few days together alone to focus on our marriage.

In the back lounge area of the plane Sasha poured us each a glass of wine.

He sat in the seat facing me with a small table between us. I placed my glass of wine on the table and stared out the small window at the clouds trying my best to avoid him.

He sighed deeply and took a sip from his glass.

"How are you?" He spoke softly.

I ignored him and continued staring out the window.

He sighed again.

"Maybe we'll do some shopping in Paris and go to an opera. How does that sound? I'm sure you can do some damage to my bank account."

I rolled my eyes at him and tried to stand from my seat.

He grabbed my arm and pulled me back down.

"Talk to me!" He shouted.

The flight attendant opened the door and peeked in.

"Is everything okay? Can I get either of you anything?"

"NO!" Sasha yelled at the attendant. "We need some privacy!"

Startled she quickly closed the door.

Sasha turned back towards me with the veins at his temple protruding.

"You're never happy are you? I give you a life that millions could only dream of and this is the thanks I get?"

"Oh, am I supposed to thank you every time you screw another one of your fan girls!" I felt the blood rushing to my face.

I thought about Sandy scolding me for not standing up for myself against Sasha.

"Oh, please. You knew what I was about when you married me. You knew there would be other women."

"Being with other women in your own time is one thing, it's humiliating when you do it in my face. Especially when you are only a few yards away from your family!"

"No one told you to follow me! You wanted to watch! I bet you enjoyed that young, supple woman giving me the pleasure that you refuse."

"Well, excuse me for not wanting you after knowing your dick has been in over half the women on earth!"

"You didn't have a problem being one of these earth women crying your way into my hotel room behind that little French boy's back. You knew exactly what you were doing with that sob story. And, as soon as you got your way you turned into just another money grabbing fame whore." His eyes became cold and mean.

"Why are you doing this to me?" I couldn't take it anymore. The tears poured down my face as I sobbed uncontrollably.

Sasha's face softened as he watched me shivering from crying so hard in the chair.

"I'm sorry." He uttered as he rose from his seat and cradled me in his arms. "I've been so stressed out with the upcoming tour and business deals, I should not have taken my frustration out on you."

I buried my face into his large chest leaving a trail of wet stains from my tears.

He lifted my chin with his hand to face him.

"I love you, Sam." He kissed my lips gently and wiped the streams of tears from my cheeks.

"Why do you need to be with these women?"

"I don't know. It's difficult to say no to them."

"Why?"

"Sam, I've been doing this for decades. Hell, before you were born was when I started this band. And, over the years my view of women changed. It wasn't always like this."

I stared confused at his admission.

He pulled me out of my seat and across the aisle.

As we settled onto the couch. He took a sip of his wine and proceeded to finish his confession.

"When we first started Derelict's Rising I'd just turned twenty years old and married my high school sweet heart, Sandy's mom. She was the only woman I'd been with and after a few years when the band started getting more popular she accompanied me on our tours." He looked down into his wine glass and breathed deeply before continuing.

"We were opening for the band Scorpion's Tale. They were iconic in the late 80's and early 90's and it was a big deal opening for them. They flew to each of their shows on a private plane and for the last show they let our band fly with them. Sandy's mom was with me and three months pregnant with her at the time. On the flight, everyone was drinking and getting high, including Sandy's mom. The lead singer of Scorpion's Tale started kissing her and I tried to stop him. She pushed me away and continued kissing him. Then, the other band members started pulling her clothes off and she let them. All I could do was sit there with my band and watch her get gang banged by all the members of Scorpion's Tale on their private plane. Afterwards, she ran off with them and got hooked on drugs really bad. She had Sandy prematurely and I had to raise her alone for two years while she went to rehab."

A few tears rolled down his cheek and he quickly wiped them away.

"After that the band started becoming more famous in the late 90's and we started outperforming Scorpion's Tale. Women threw themselves at us. I mean they wanted to do everything. Women would sneak into my hotel, mothers with their daughters, backstage girls doing things to me and each other that blew my mind, and I could not understand why. Then, I realized I was a form of escapism for them. They wanted to live for a few moments in a fantasy that took them out of their ordinary lives. Being with them is not for my benefit, it's for theirs. That's what happened with Sandy's mom. She wanted to be in this fantasy world and saw them as a way to escape. And, the record label has also been pressuring me to be this lady's man to continue selling out shows and merchandise."

After listening to his confession, I started to understand the pressures he faced living up to this figure that everyone looked up to.

He faced me and stroked my hair.

"Sam, I love you. I really do. But, you have to understand that there will always be other women. I will give you everything you desire and do my best to be discreet, but as long as I am touring there will be other women. Can you live with this?"

A lump formed in my throat and it became hard to speak.

I wasn't sure if I could continue being with him this way, but I didn't have any other alternative. So, I nodded my head and whispered.

"Yes."

I missed Paris.

Only this time, I could afford to shop in the stores that I would pass by before only being able to peer in the windows and dream.

Sasha promised that these few days would be for us and that he would not even look at another woman.

He booked us a suite in a beautiful hotel that looked onto the Eiffel Tower.

I laid on the bed and ran the tips of my fingers over the baccarat diamond necklace Sasha surprised me with as we entered the room.

I closed its suede box and laid back onto the soft comforter.

"Do you like it?" Sasha stood nude in the bathroom doorway. His manhood swaying between his large muscular thighs as he walked towards the bed.

"I love it." I didn't even try to sound excited.

I honestly didn't know how I felt. After everything we'd been through with his infidelity, the necklace felt like a token for my cooperation.

I just laid back on the bed as he climbed over me. He kissed me and when I did not kiss him back, he kissed me harder.

He sat up and stared at me as if I were something he owned.

I didn't move.

A sinister smile spread across his face making the corners of his eyes wrinkle giving him a villainous expression.

He yanked my skirt up hastily pulled my panties to the side and shoved himself inside of me.

I stared at the details of the moldings on the ceiling. The designs was delicate and beautiful.

Sasha grunted deep and low as his warmth filled me. I shoved him off of me as I stood from the bed and made my way into the bathroom.

Thankfully, Sasha got a vasectomy after I had Sadie. I loved our daughter but I couldn't bear the thought of having another child.

As I sat on the toilet, I stated thinking of Fred.

Suddenly, I had the overwhelming need to see him.

I came out of the bathroom and Sasha just laid on his back with his eyes closed. I could tell he wasn't asleep but I did not care. I grabbed my purse and shoes then left the room.

I don't know what came over me. Normally, I would never leave Sasha's side especially late at night. But, I needed to go to Montmartre.

I requested a car from the hotel concierge and it was waiting for me as soon as I made my way to the exit.

My heart pounded as the car made its way up the hill.

The driver pulled up in front of the familiar apartment building that I once called home. As I climbed out of the car, I just stood on the sidewalk. The nostalgia was overwhelming.

The car pulled away and I did not know what to do

next.

Standing there I heard music from a bar just up the street. The sound was familiar and I was drawn to it.

I paid my admission and entered the smoke filled bar room. The lights were dimmed and in the spotlight on the stage there was Fred with his black hair slicked back into a low bun, hunched over the mic stand singing out of tune.

His frame was still thin but he had a small bloated belly that protruded out from under his shirt.

I walked to the stage and stood directly in front of him. We made eye contact but he didn't acknowledge me.

He closed his eyes and continued his crooning into the microphone.

I quietly sat at the bar and waited for the set to finish.

While the band was still playing, Fred just stepped off of the stage and walked drunkenly towards me.

He plopped onto the barstool next to me.

"Buy me a drink. You can afford it now." He still didn't look at me.

I handed the bartender 20 euros and he dutifully mixed Fred his drink.

Fred took a long sip from the glass.

"How are you?" I could see how he was doing, but I needed to say something to break the silence.

"Well, not as good as you." He looked at me from the corner of his eyes still refusing to look at me.

"Fred, I'm sorry."

"Oh, fuck you!" Now, he faced me as he slammed his fist against the bar. "You could have saved yourself a trip if that's what you came to say to me."

He took another sip this time spilling some of it onto his shirt.

"What do you want, Sam? Huh? You want to pity fuck

me. Because I'll take a pity fuck, even from you."

He shoved his hand between my thighs and tried to pull my thong to the side. I wrestled his hand away.

He sniffed his fingertips.

"Smells like you already pity fucked someone."

I realized this was a mistake.

Seeing Fred in this state made me feel responsible for ruining his life.

I stood from the bar to leave after being humiliated then Fred grabbed my arm.

"Sam, don't ever fucking come back here again."

I turned toward the door and it took all of my might not to breakdown and cry.

My legs trembled as I made my way down the street to a low wall I could sit on. And, I let the tears run freely down my face.

"Sam, get in."

Sasha's voice startled me as he sat in the back of a black town car. I didn't even notice the car drive up. The driver held the door open for me to climb in.

I wiped the tear stains from my cheeks.

"How did you know I was here?"

"When you walked out I had a feeling you would come here." He looked at me disappointed.

"Sasha, he's ruined. I ruined everything for him." The tears started to well up in my eyes again.

"Sam, you did not ruin him." Sasha rolled his eyes.

"You ruined him too when you punched him in front of all those people!"

"Really, Sam! Really!" Sasha's voice raised and the driver glanced back at us in the rearview mirror.

"Sasha, he lost everything because of you!"

"No, Sam! He lost everything because he charged towards you violently as if he was going to harm you and

I stopped him! Or, did you forget that part!" Sasha's face turned red with rage."Honestly, any man who does something like that to a woman deserves to be ruined. And, I'd do it again. But, somehow I became the bad guy in this story."

He was right, but after seeing Fred in such bad shape it didn't stop me from feeling responsible in some way.

The car pulled in front of our hotel. I climbed out and the driver closed the door leaving Sasha inside.

He wouldn't look at me as the driver climbed into the car and drove away leaving me standing in front of the hotel alone.

I heard my cellphone chime and saw it was a text message from my sister.

Mom died this morning.

Part IV: Lexi

10

"Watch your step, miss." One of the yacht crewmen extended his hand to help me onto the platform.

"Oh, and you must remove your shoes before stepping onto the deck."

I wrestled my feet out of the espadrilles I put on in a rush to get to the airport.

Sasha called me out of the blue and demanded I be on a plane within three hours to Saint-Tropez.

While I enjoyed being out of the typical gloomy foggy London, I did not like being rushed.

The crew member continued escorting me up a small staircase.

I could hear Sasha's deep English accent as I made it to the top of the stairs. He was standing at a small bar area talking to the band's guitar player Laney and a young woman with long red hair and a tattooed sleeve on her left arm.

Laney draped his arm around her waist, but she was completely absorbed into Sasha that she did not return Laney's embrace.

When Sasha saw me he turned his back to them and enveloped me into his large chest. When he kissed me a glare of hate flashed in the young woman's eyes. I could tell she was going to be a problem.

"I missed you." He whispered in my ear.

"I missed you, too."

"Let me introduce you to everyone." Sasha grabbed my hand and walked past Laney and the red head guiding me to a lounge area where a few other people were gathered.

He led me to a beautiful woman of Indian decent. She had purple curly hair braided into a mohawk with the curls falling over to one side.

"This is Veronica. She's one of the best agents out there. I told her about the song you wrote for me."

Veronica stepped towards me and reached out her hand with an air of superiority which made me feel intimidated in her presence.

I took her hand and did my best to not show my insecurity.

"I love that song." She tried to soften her approach to ease my intimidation.

I managed to squeak out a "thank you" and was immediately mortified at my nervousness.

"Sasha spoke with me about working with you on writing a few songs for the newer artists I am representing."

"Really! I would love that." I could feel my face warming with excitement.

I could not believe this was happening.

"Okay. Here's my card and let's meet up sometime back in London. It was good to see you again Sasha."

They kissed on the cheek and she left down the side staircase.

"See, I told you I would help you."

I planted the biggest kiss onto Sasha's lips.

"Thank you so much!"

"Of course. Now, let me get you a drink to celebrate."

As the day went on, many people showed up and it was a very nice gathering with a mix of artists, billionaire businessmen, and beautiful women. This was the type of crowd I always envisioned myself being a part of.

Many of them told me how much they enjoyed the song I co-wrote with Sasha and Sha. I noticed Casey rolling her eyes each time I was complemented.

Casey and Laney followed Sasha around the yacht with Laney introducing himself to everyone Sasha spoke to. His intentions made many uncomfortable as they only acknowledged him out of respect for Sasha.

Around midnight the only people left on the yacht other than the staff were two of the billionaire businessmen, Casey and Laney, myself, Sasha and a few women in their 20's who were invited later.

One of the crew members handed the women and Casey bikinis and led them to the lower deck to change.

I took the elevator with Sasha up to the owners suite.

It was nice to finally be alone with him.

As soon as we entered the room he wrapped his arms around my waist and pressed his himself against my lower back. He leaned in and pressed his lips against my ear.

"Why don't we put on our swimsuits and go have some fun at the pool below?"

"Okay?" It seemed he was insinuating something.

"I want to see you let loose tonight."

I stood still waiting for him to clarify, loose.

"I want to watch all those girls lick you all over."

He slid his hand between my thighs and pulled my

panties to the side and slowly stroked me.

My body stiffened as he continued gently rubbing back and forth.

"I want you to know that no matter what happens tonight, it's you and me. It will always be you and me. You are my number one and always will be."

The yacht began pulling forward away from the dock towards the open waters. Sasha decided to anchor away from the port for more privacy and to keep the paparazzi who had been stalking the port all day from taking pictures.

He pulled his hand up and guided me to a vanity desk with a rectangle suede jewelry box on top.

He opened the box to reveal a long necklace of large champagne golden South Sea pearls with matching earrings.

The cold touch of the pearls caused goosebumps to form on my chest as he laid the heavy necklace around my neck. As he clasped the closure I glanced at my reflection in the mirror and watched the iridescent colors dance with each slight movement.

He kissed the nape of my neck.

"You are the most beautiful woman."

I stood there stunned and at a loss for words.

Sasha's eyes met mine in the mirror's reflection and he smiled gently.

"Do you like it?"

"Yes." I ran my hand over the cold, smooth pearls.

Suddenly, Sasha spun me around to face him and he kissed me deeply.

"Let's change into our swimsuits and head down to the pool."

As we stepped from the elevator onto the lower deck all of

the girls were topless or fully nude and splashing in the pool.

The two billionaires stood by watching the girls with delight and discussing who was their favorite.

Laney and Casey sat on the edge of a lounge chair near the sauna room.

Laney stared at the two billionaires intently while Casey tried to look aloof with her head cocked back and holding a champagne glass.

As soon as she noticed Sasha and I walking in her body came to attention.

"You guys having fun." Sasha said to Laney as he noticed his defeated expression.

"Yeah, we're good just hanging out." Laney tried to sound upbeat.

Casey sat quietly with her chest out showing her cleavage in a red bikini with a padded pushup top. She stared intently at Sasha with no acknowledgement of me standing next to him.

"Whoa! Nice necklace Lexi! Are those South Sea pearls?" Laney put his hand up pointing at my necklace.

"Thank you. Sasha just gave it to me."

At this point Casey glanced at my necklace and then met my eyes with snare of envy.

"So, are you two joining the party in the pool?" Sasha darted a glance at Casey which made Laney's body stiffen awkwardly.

"Nah. I better take Casey back to the room before it gets too x-rated down here."

Laney stood up and reached for Casey's hand to guide her away but she pulled away from him and stayed seated.

"Um. Casey, you coming?" Laney sounded worried at her reaction to him.

"Let's stay and have some fun." She looked up at Sasha.

This was my first time hearing her speak in her sultry British accent.

"I don't think you want this type of fun." Laney reached for her hand again and she pulled away.

A menaced look flashed across his face.

"Hey. Why don't we have some more champagne and see how the night goes." Sasha was trying to defuse the situation but it was too late.

I quickly stepped aside as Laney grabbed Casey's arm and pulled her onto her feet. She wrestled with him. Everyone by the pool noticed the commotion and stopped splashing in the pool to watch.

Sasha stepped between them and pulled Casey from Laney's grasp.

"You've had too much to drink, Laney." Sasha put his hands up as if to calm a wild animal.

"Let Casey stay and have some fun while you go up and sleep it off."

"Fuck you Sasha! You think you're so much better than everybody. You ain't shit!" Saliva sprayed from Laney's mouth and onto Sasha's face.

Sasha wiped his face and grabbed Laney's shoulders with his large hands.

"Laney, go up to your room, now. We both know this won't end well for you." Sasha spoke sternly and with complete authority.

Laney stared back at Sasha with pure hate in his eyes. He snatched away from him and walked hurried and ashamed toward the elevator.

The hair stood up on my arms at the ordeal and before I could console Sasha, Casey pushed past me and buried her small face into his chest with tears streaming down her cheeks.

"Thank you." Her voice was now soft and sheepish.

"It's okay." Sasha wrapped his arms around her and took her champagne glass. "Let me refresh your drink."

They walked together to the bar, leaving me standing alone.

A few girls in the pool noticed Casey's damsel in distress maneuver and snickered at me standing there like a third wheel.

The pool party quickly turned x-rated.

Casey didn't leave Sasha's side the whole night. At the bar next to the pool I sat on one side of him and she sat on the other.

She continuously found ways to distract him and take his attention away from me, forcing him to turn his head towards her and his back towards me.

The back of the yacht was open revealing the stars reflection on the water and a view of Saint Tropez in the distance, lit and bustling with disco lights on the smaller yachts who were having their own parties.

I ran my hand over the pearl necklace to remind myself that I was special to Sasha and no matter how hard Casey tried, she would never be in my position.

As I pretended to be uninterested in Sasha and Casey's conversation, I watched as one of the billionaires sat on the edge of the pool with his feet in the water. He looked about 60 years old with a clean shaven head and a normal build.

He kicked his feet up splashing two topless blondes then moving his finger in a come hither motion at them. They smiled and swam toward him. He pull down the front of his swim trunks to reveal an average size manhood surrounded by dark curly hair.

He placed his hands on their heads and pulled them to him.

The other billionaire who was in his 50s was muscular with blond hair gelled back into a ponytail laid back on a lounge chair. Three women laid on the lounge chair next to him performing on each other. He didn't engage with them, but watched them while occasionally stroking himself.

He glanced in my direction and caught me staring. I looked away but it was too late, he continued to stare at me while stroking himself.

Feeling uncomfortable I turned to Sasha who now had Casey standing in-between his thighs. They stared knowingly into each others' eyes. She whispered in his ear then glanced at me.

Sasha turned to me and kissed my cheek.

"Hey, let's all go into the sauna."

He stood up and grasped our hand in each of his guiding us into the large sauna room.

The moist heat from the wood paneled room formed into droplets of moisture on my bare skin.

Sasha set us on a large wooden bench and poured cold water on the hot stones which made a loud noise and formed a cloud of steam that quickly dissipated into the air.

Casey with her eyes locked on Sasha removed her bikini with ease while I struggled with a knot that would not budge on the bikini string at the nape of my neck.

As Sasha approached the bench, Casey jumped to her feet and wrapped her tattooed arm around his shoulders and kissed him passionately.

He sat on the bench next to me and she straddled his lap then shoved her tongue into his mouth. I just sat there awkwardly watching them unsure of what to do.

It's not as if this was my first threesome with Sasha and another woman.

But, Casey overpowered him and consumed him so that there was no room for me to participate.

Sasha did not seem to notice nor care that I was being left out.

Casey pulled down the front of his swim trunks revealing his manhood and shoved it into herself.

She moved slowly at first, then her rhythm quickened as she moved up and down on his lap.

Sasha breathed deeply and stared intently into her eyes. This was how he to looked at me when we made love.

I watched as he slowly fell for with her.

She released a soft, feminine moan and threw her head back with her red hair damp from the moist heat leaving stripes of wet lines as it swayed over her back.

The necklace I wore began collecting large pools of water that ran down and pooled between my thighs.

As I watched them coming closer to climax, I removed my heavy wet pearl necklace and laid it on the bench. Then, I left unnoticed out of the room.

I felt the eyes of the pool guests and yacht crew watching me walk awkwardly to the elevator.

11

"Hey, where did you go last night?"

I awoke to find Sasha hovering over me. It was obvious he didn't sleep last night with his bloodshot eyes staring down at me.

I barely remembered anything after leaving the pool party last night. I was holding a bottle of champagne which spilled onto the comforter and dried tear stains laid on my cheeks.

I also still couldn't loosen the knot at the nape of my neck from the bikini, so it set twisted around my chest, not covering my breasts. It was also the only thing I was still wearing.

Sasha continued to stare down at me concerned as his brows furrowed.

"How about you freshen up a bit and join me on the sun deck for some breakfast."

I sat up nodding my head and suddenly felt dizzy from the heaviness of my head that I almost fell backwards onto the pillow.

Sasha quickly kissed my forehead then left the room.

I pulled my aching limbs from the plush bed and climbed to my feet, stumbled to the vanity and saw the pearl necklace placed carefully on top of the velvet box.

I felt ashamed for leaving it in the sauna last night.

I saw my reflection in the mirror and I barely recognized myself. My skin was so dry that small lines formed on my forehead and corners of my eyes. Dark, deep set circles around my eyes made me look sickly.

What was happening to me?

This lifestyle was definitely taking its toll. I needed to pull myself together.

I removed the knotted bikini top by squeezing my head through the straps and went into the bathroom to wash, exfoliate, and most importantly moisturize.

Tropical jazz played from the speakers as I made my way to a small lounging area near the jacuzzi.

Sasha set back on a lounge sipping a mimosa.

He looked relaxed with his light blue shirt buttoned down to reveal the soft dark curly hairs on his chest and white shorts that came just above his knee. I realized I've never seen him in shorts before. He normally wore dark colors and fitted jeans to show off is toned legs.

He heard me approaching from behind and sat up looking back at me.

I decided to wear a white halter knee length dress and pulled my braids into a chic bun to match the atmosphere. I also made sure to wear my pearl necklace.

Sasha's eyes approved of my look.

"You look absolutely beautiful."

He kissed my hand then pulled me down so he could kiss my lips.

The troubles of last night faded away.

I laid onto the lounge next to him and a crew member

handed me a mimosa. On a small coffee table in front of us was platter with eggs Benedict, lobster, and various fruits.

We were still anchored out at the sea, so I could see Saint Tropez in the distance as people walked along the dock looking at the yachts and eating at the small cafes.

I realized at that moment just how lucky I was.

Who would have guessed that me, a black girl from Atlanta, would be sitting here on a super yacht, wearing expensive jewelry, drinking champagne, and in love with the most attractive iconic rock star in the world. This was a once in a lifetime experience that only few will have.

"The others took the speed boat to the port, so we have the whole yacht to ourselves all morning."

I leaned over and kissed him.

"I love you." I whispered in his ear.

"I love you, more."

Salt water entered my mouth as Sasha and I made love in the sea.

He held onto a silver handrail from the yacht's lowered dock as I straddled my legs around his waist and moved in rhythm on him.

He moved my white bikini top to the side to reveal my breasts and did the same with my bottoms.

His biceps bulged as he anchored all of my weight on him and kept us from sinking into the depths of the deep waters.

Every few minutes a wave gently rose and washed over our heads.

His large deep dark eyes stared intensely into mine. With a stoic expression he didn't wince once as he held our bodies steady in the moving water.

My body warmed in the cool water as pleasure rose

inside me. The pressure built up so quickly my head became heavy and fell gently to the side.

Sasha firmed his grip on the handrail as my body began to twitch with tiny orgasmic explosions.

Then, the pressure released all at once leaving me so exhausted I no longer had the strength to hold on to him. My arms and legs felt weightless allowing a wave to carry me away.

Sasha quickly let go of the rail to catch me and pulled me back into him.

He pressed his lips hard against mine and he tasted like the sea as he kissed me.

I was madly in love with him and felt like the only girl in the world, but that moment was shattered when the sound of the speedboat boomed as it moved towards the yacht.

We quickly climbed onto the dock and I fixed my bikini.

As the speedboat drew closer I saw the two billionaires with three of the girls from last night and Casey holding a duffle bag in her lap.

The boat pulled up to the lower dock and a crew member began assisting everyone off the boat. Sasha stood on the dock greeting everyone while I made my way to the bar by the pool sighing in annoyance at the sight of Casey.

I thought she had gone back to Laney.

She was wearing a pair of black designer shades and a tiny red halter dress which revealed that she was not wearing underwear as she stepped onto the dock.

She whispered something to Sasha as they embraced each other.

When she saw me sitting at the bar her expression became tense.

Sasha took her bag and walked behind her as she

moved past me without acknowledging my presence.

Sasha handed the duffle bag to a crew person and Casey followed them along with the other guests to the elevator.

He glanced at me with a guilty expression then walked towards me with his lips pursed.

He kissed my cheek and inhaled deeply.

"What's going on?" My heart pounded in my chest.

"Casey is flying back to London with you tomorrow." He stared intently waiting for my response.

"Okay?"

"Laney is kicking her out of his home and she has no where to stay, so she will be staying with you in London for a while."

"WHAT!?"

12

"One, two, three! Bam! Bam! Bam!"

Casey and two of her girlfriends were in the back garden dancing.

They set up her cell phone on a tripod and recorded themselves doing a dance routine to upload on some new social media site everyone was crazy about.

Since Casey was featured in gossip magazines and blogs for being the other woman and breaking up Jani and Laney's marriage, she had amassed a huge following.

It was only a few days since she moved in and her stuff was everywhere.

She always had friends over and they were loud and never cleaned up after themselves. The house also constantly smelled of burnt herbs.

I spent most of the time sulking in my room.

I even had a keyed lock put on my bedroom door to keep them from snooping through my things whenever I was away.

Whenever I did venture out of my room, they just ignored me and acted as if I was't present.

Before, I thought I was so depressed and lonely being here alone for so long, but now I would give anything to have that loneliness back.

"I've got to get out of here." I murmured to myself.

I wanted to get a hotel room for some peace, but Sasha text me that he was coming over later.

I read online that Sam's mother passed away, so I assumed he wanted to see me and Casey before he left for America to attend the funeral.

While Casey spent all day dancing with her friends and slacking off as usual. I cleaned most of the downstairs area.

Somehow, I became the live-in housekeeper for Casey and her friends.

As the time for Sasha's visit neared, Casey had her friends vacate the house.

We both stayed in our rooms to prepare ourselves for Sasha's arrival.

Just as I was coming out of my room, I heard the vacuum cleaner running which was odd because I had already vacuumed and cleaned everything earlier.

I made my way down the stairs and Casey was standing still at the front door with the vacuum running. Before I could confront her, Sasha came through the door and as soon as he saw Casey, she shut off the vacuum.

"Hey! I just finished cleaning." I felt a stab in my heart as she lied to him.

I was the one who cleaned and she was trying to take credit for it.

"Look at you! My little housekeeper!" Sasha lifted her up and she straddled her legs around his waist and they kissed.

"Excuse me. No, I cleaned everything while you and your friends were dancing in the back yard all day!" I felt the blood rushing to my cheeks.

"What is your problem? She's been so mean to me since I've been here." Casey jumped back onto the ground and pouted her lips.

"Lexi, try to get along. Casey is just trying to help out with the cleaning." Sasha comforted Casey.

"But, she didn't help. She just stood there running the vacuum pretending to clean."

"Look! I came to spend some time with you two before I leave for America. Can we get along, please?" Sasha gave me a stern, disapproving glance.

I didn't know what else to say as it seemed Casey was the new attraction and could do no wrong.

I realized this relationship was coming to an end and I needed to get my song writing career solidified soon.

I decided I needed to be proactive and sent the agent Sasha introduced me to, Veronica, a text message offering to buy her lunch to discuss writing for the singers she represented.

She replied quickly and said she had an up and coming singer from South Africa she wanted me to meet.

We agreed to meet at a small cafe just after the lunch crowds died down giving us some quietness to speak.

I made sure to arrive first and grabbed a table in a quiet corner near the large window.

I spotted her walking down the sidewalk.

Her hair was different, dark brown with honey blond tips. She wore it out in a wild curly afro letting it sway freely as she walked.

I envied her bold style as she wore a yellow button up shirt with red gingham tight fitted pants, and large army boots.

She was so confident, I felt slightly intimidated at that

moment.

She saw me in the window just before entering the cafe and smiled at me with a little wave.

This immediately made me feel at ease.

I stood to shake her hand and she wrapped her warm hand around mine.

"I am so glad you contacted me! I was going through the songs Sasha sent me that you wrote and there is one that a singer I represent would be a good fit for." She got right to business before even sitting down.

"Great! Which one did you like?"

"The one called Star Reacher. The singer's name is Sundries and when I showed her the lyrics she feel in love. Would you be available to meet in the studio in a few months to work with her?"

"Yes! I would love to!" I immediately felt embarrassed for sounding too eager and excited.

"Okay. I'll text you the details."

There was a moment of awkward silence.

Veronica sipped her tea and I pretended to watch the pedestrians crossing the street.

We made eye contact and I smiled nervously.

I could tell she wanted to say something, so I just patiently waited for her to let it out.

"So, how did you meet Sasha?" Her large brown eyes widened with interest.

"We met at one of his concerts when I was with Sha."

"I heard you were the one who introduced him to Sha and that's how they collaborated on the song you co-wrote. So, how did you know Sasha before? Come on spill the tea, Lexi."

I felt the warmth of embarrassment grow in my cheeks as she leaned in.

"Um. Sam his current wife invited me backstage and I

brought Sha with me."

"Oh! So, you were there when that French singer from the opening band got knocked out by Sasha!" Her eyes grew even wider with excitement.

"I was." I felt ashamed gossiping about that night with Veronica.

"Wait! So, you are friends with his wife!" She sat back looking at me with disdain.

"Well, it's more complicated than that."

She stared waiting for me to explain.

"Sam and I were roommates years ago when she was with Craig and I was with Johnny from the band Death of Love. We were never really close friends. She stabbed me in the back a lot of times and somehow I ended up becoming close with Sasha."

"Does Sam know you're with him?"

I looked down at my lap.

"Oh my Goodness! She knows!" Veronica stared bewildered with her mouth agape in disbelief.

"It's really more complicated than it seems."

"Girl! Complicated is an understatement for this."

I felt ashamed as I walked home.

The meeting went so well at first and I knew that things were going to get better for my career. But, I didn't expect to disclose so much private information about myself and Sasha.

Veronica made me feel like a home wrecker and bad friend to Sam. But, Sam was never really a friend to me.

She always used me as a way for her to get with whatever rock star she was into at the moment. There were so many times she stabbed me in the back and manipulated our so-called friendship. I shouldn't feel guilty at all for being with Sasha.

I was not doing anything that Sam would not do to me if the roles were reversed.

I opened the front door and was surprised by the silence. There had not been any silence here since Casey moved in.

This was good because I did not need anymore frustration.

I decided to relax and try to take my mind off of the grilling I got from Veronica. So, I grabbed a bottle of wine from the now sparse collection since Casey and her friends devoured most of it.

I made my way upstairs to my room to enjoy the wine and a movie on my laptop in peace.

I realized my bedroom door was unlocked. I thought maybe I was so nervous about my meeting with Veronica that I likely forgot to lock it.

As I entered my room I noticed my closet door wide open and my books laying on the floor.

I dropped the glass and bottle of wine and ran over to the closet.

I flipped through all of the books I hid my jewelry in and everything was gone.

Whoever broke into my room went through all of my stuff and took purses, shoes, clothes, and worst of all my jewelry stash I was keeping for security if I needed to pawn them.

The room felt like it was spinning and I could barely hold myself up as I began hyperventilating from the shock.

"Why did you have them hidden in old books?" Sasha held the books in each hand looking puzzled as he examined the square holes I had cut into the middle of the pages that once contained my jewelry.

"I was afraid of someone finding them." I sat on the edge of the bed watching Sasha look through my burglarized closet.

"Well, that didn't work out so well." He gave me a disapproving glance. "They took a lot of stuff. Lexi, I could have helped you get a safe for your room. It would have been a lot safer than this."

I lowered my head in shame.

"I know it was one of Casey's friends, or even Casey herself. She knew I had the pearl necklace here. And, no one else comes here. She always has people over to record dance routines and random stuff for her to post on social media."

"What? Casey should not be recording anything here let alone posting it to social media. I made that very clear to her."

Sasha sighed in frustration.

I was counting on pawning most of those items to buy a small apartment. The pearl necklace Sasha gave me alone was worth over $100,000, but now that dream was over. And, the thought of this made me cry.

Sasha sat next to me on the bed and put his arm around my shoulders pulling me into him.

I buried my face in his large chest.

"Since you didn't properly secure your jewelry the insurance won't cover it. But, we will recover your things. I know a really good private detective." Sasha lifted my face to his. "You are my number one and when I get back from America, I'm going to take care of this. Everything will be fine."

As he kissed me, I could not shake a deep feeling that everything was about to get a lot worse.

Part V: Sam

13

"I'm surprised she showed up."

"I know. She's to busy living that fancy life in England and left her poor sister here alone to take care of their momma."

"And, she showed up with a whole entourage. Do they really need a PR person and bodyguards at a funeral?"

"Remember how she treated that boy DJ. Left him in a mess. I think he might show up for the wake."

"Oh. And, don't forget about her friend Sophie. She didn't even show up for her wedding after Sophie was there for her all those years."

"Yeah. When they were kids Sophie was the only one who was her friend because no one else wanted to deal with that selfish Samantha."

As I made my way down the aisle of the church at my mother's wake, I couldn't help but overhear everyone's whispered opinions of me.

I tried my best to ignore the judgements, but they were all true.

I spotted Sasha sitting at the far end of the front row.

He couldn't appear to be an unsupportive husband at the funeral of the mother-in-law he never cared to meet, so he insisted on coming with me for moral support.

And, knowing the press would be here, Renea was definitely present to manage everything.

As I approached my mother's casket, I was taken aback as she didn't look the same as when I last saw her.

An oversized dress suit swallowed her frail body. Makeup that was too light for her complexion was caked on her boney face. And, a curly auburn-colored synthetic wig sat crooked on her head.

It was so sad knowing this was the last image everyone would have of her.

I stood frozen over her body in the fancy overpriced casket. I never knew how to communicate with her and this moment didn't make it any easier.

But, I knew everyone was watching me closely so I had to say something.

"Good bye."

It was awkward being in my childhood home.

The small three bedroom house was in need of a lot of care. As I noticed the wood shingles and window sills rotting with termite damage.

Being in Griffin, Georgia was a different world from the one I lived in today with Sasha.

My sister decided to have everyone from the funeral come to my mom's home afterwards. It was the usual potluck style with everyone bringing their own southern food dish.

Most of the men gathered in the backyard facing a cow farm. I couldn't stand the smell of the cow manure. It made me wonder how I lived with it everyday growing up.

The women congregated inside in the small living room that doubled as the dining area.

The dining table was crowded with various tinfoil covered platters which made the whole house smell of collard greens, pork, candid yams, and fried chicken.

Everyone consoled my sister while barely acknowledging my existence in the room.

Sasha was very intrigued by the environment and all of the women surrounded him as he inquired about life in rural Georgia.

While Sasha entertained everyone I decided to visit my old room.

A waft of mold escaped as I opened the door to the small room.

Boxes of various items were stacked on my old bed collecting dust. The room was used as a storage for all the forgotten items my mom hoarded over the past decades.

My dresser that my mom found sitting on the side of the road in a wealthy neighborhood had a thick layer of dust caked on it and I could barely see my reflection in the mirror from it rarely being cleaned.

I opened the top draw and found some old magazines I collected as a teenager.

I pulled them out and sat them on top of the dresser.

As I sorted through the teen and entertainment magazines, I froze when I saw a rock n' roll magazine with Derelict's Rising on the cover.

They were so young in the cover photo with smooth skin and slim bodies.

Sasha was always muscular with broad shoulders but he was a lot leaner back then.

I felt nostalgic suddenly as I recalled being a huge fan of the band as a teenager. I lusted over Sasha and had fantasies of being with him.

He was what inspired me to become a rock n' roll groupie in the first place.

I opened the magazine to the band's interview.

There were candid photos of Sasha sitting on a couch backstage surrounded by provocatively dressed young women vying for his attention.

The interviewer discussed the rumors of Sasha's orgies with several groupies at a time. He boasted about his virility in the interview, it made me laugh at how cheesy and self absorbed he was. But, at the time I thought he was such a macho man.

It's amazing how differently I viewed him now.

"Is this your room?"

I turned to see Sasha's large frame in the doorway. The door was so narrow he had to turn sideways to enter the room.

"Yeah, look what I found."

I held up the magazine showing him the cover with him and the band.

"No way!" He laughed and grabbed the mold stained magazine studying the cover. "We were so young here."

"I was so in love with you as a teen." I revealed.

"WAS in love?" He grinned at me pretending to be offended.

"You know what I mean."

He laid the magazine on the dusty dresser and pulled me to him, wrapping his large muscular arms around me.

"And, who would have thought I'd be standing in your room as your husband."

"I guess wishes do come true."

As he kissed me I was transported to the teenager who dreamed of this and prayed that I would one day be with this man.

He shoved the boxes off the bed onto the floor and laid me on my back, pressing my body against the mattress as he climbed on top of me.

The scent of mold and dust surrounded us, but I did not care, I wanted him.

He pushed his long, thick tongue past my lips, kissing me deeply.

I missed these moments.

He pulled up my dress and moved my panties to the side, then gently massaged between my thighs.

Then, he hurriedly unzipped his pants and entered me.

I relaxed as he grind his pelvis against mine and the sensations of pleasure soon followed.

He stared intensely into my eyes and I felt his love for me. Something I had not felt from him in a long time.

I lifted my face to his and pressed my lips onto his lips.

His body began to quiver and he pressed all of his weight onto me pushing me further into the mattress.

I didn't know why, but I wanted to give myself to him just as I'd imagined so many years before sitting in this room praying to be with him one day.

His manhood became firmer and I felt his warmth inside me as he poured himself into me pressing his pelvis firmly against mine.

He kissed me with moist heat gasping from his mouth.

"I love you." He whispered.

He laid his head beside mine resting his chin on my shoulder, then I saw the bedroom door open. I caught a glimpse of my sister as she hurriedly closed the door being careful not to make a noise.

I began to feel uncomfortable being there, but I did not want to let go of this moment with Sasha.

So, I laid still, closed my eyes and inhaled the dust and mold that filled the air.

We tried our best to sneak out of my old room without anyone noticing, but with the room falling silent as soon as we entered suggested they knew what we were up to.

But, something else seemed to hold everyone's attention as they whispered and avoided eye contact with us.

Renae turned from the television and looked at us with an expression of horror frozen on her face.

My sister stared at me with a small smile as she turned up the volume on the television.

It was a celebrity gossip entertainment show reporting on a breaking news story. With closer inspection there was an image of the St. John's Wood London home Sasha was hiding Lexi in.

My throat tightened and my skin crawled when I saw the headline 'Sasha's Love Harem" in bold letters on the screen.

14

Craig: I'm sorry for your loss. I saw that you recently lost your mother. We'll be in London next week to get ready for the show. Give me a call. I'd like to see you.

I stared at the text. Rereading it several times as I contemplated replying.

Sadie and Sean laid sound asleep next to me on a blanket in the grass.

It was a beautiful sunny day and I wanted to enjoy it.

I kissed Sadie softly on the cheek, thankful they didn't have to witness the ordeal Sasha and I went through with the paparazzi chasing us and then waiting for us outside our estate here in Sussex.

Thank goodness we flew private and did not have to walk through a crowded airport.

I was glad to be here in privacy with nothing but nature surrounding us.

Sasha and I avoided each other the past week with him in one wing of the estate and me in the other.

He spent most of his time in his office, taking meetings

with his lawyers and trying to get the media to stop reporting on his harem story.

I had a desire to see Craig, but could not bear to leave Sadie and Sean during this trying time.

My phone chimed and to my surprise it was Jani.

Jani: Hey! Sorry about your mother passing. I am here for you. Let's do lunch soon.

I had not heard from her since the embarrassing scene at the charity concert in London. I guess with Sasha's cheating scandal she felt less inferior to me now.

I decided not to text her right back.

I was still Sasha's wife and inferior to no one.

"Oh you poor thing! What a roller coaster you've been on lately."

Jani squeezed me in her embrace as she stroked my hair.

"It's fine. How have you been?" I stood still waiting for her to stop petting me.

"Oh! Let's not worry about me. I'm managing."

Jani breezed past me toward the bar lounge overlooking the outdoor pool.

She walked behind the mahogany bar and helped herself to a bottle of Burgundy wine.

As she poured the wine into two wine glasses she seemed too comfortable which made me feel uneasy. I realized this subtle trespassing was a challenge to dominate my space and station in my own home.

She extended a glass to me and walked from behind the bar brushing past me to sit on the plush couch facing the pool and landscaping.

"Come sit down and tell me everything." Jani patted the

space next to her.

I hesitantly sat next to her avoiding her stare.

"Well, um.." I began then she cut me off.

"You know I could have been the lady of this estate." She took a sip of wine. "Once upon a time, there was a moment between Sasha and I. But, as you know he LOVES the ladies and I respected myself too much to accept this part of him."

My shoulders slumped forward and tension began to build slowly in my head.

I took a deep breath and turned towards Jani, but before I could speak she looked past me and her eyes lit up.

"Look who it is. We were just discussing you." She flipped her freshly blown out blonde hair.

I turned to see Sasha holding Sadie and looking shocked to see Jani sitting on the couch.

"Sadie was crying, I think she's hungry." Sasha approached me with Sadie, then Jani sprung from the couch extending her arms and collecting Sadie from Sasha's grasp.

"Oh! You've gotten so big!" Jani kissed Sadie on the cheek. Sadie with an annoyed expression held up her tiny hands in defense pushing Jani's face away from her.

As Sadie started crying in protest to Jani's unwanted affection, I quickly walked over and took her from Jani. She buried her face into my neck and whimpered.

Trying to save face, Jani then wrapped her arms around Sasha's neck giving him a hug that lasted a few seconds too long.

"I was telling your wife how I almost ended up with you."

Sasha stood aback, pulling away from Jani.

"What?" He stared at her confused.

"You know we had a little something going on back in

the day. But, I made the error of choosing Laney over you." She laid her hand onto Sasha's chest.

"Um...uh." Sasha stuttered in confusion at Jani's ambush of memories.

I really did not want to deal with any more of this so I carried Sadie into the adjoining room to feed her.

I looked into Sadie's large green eyes. She stared back at me concerned over the uncomfortable situation with Jani.

It's amazing with her being so young she could pick up on the bad vibes.

She paused feeding and laid stunned at the sound of commotion coming from the other room.

Suddenly, I heard Sasha protesting.

Holding Sadie close, I rushed into the room to find Sasha shoving Jani from his lap.

"Jani! It's time for you to go!" Sasha's voice boomed with rage.

"All of you men are the same! You make love to me one day, then the next I'm suddenly no good for you!"

"What? That was over a decade ago!" Sasha signaled for the housekeeper to notify security.

I stood at a safe distance with Sadie and watched as Sasha struggled to keep Jani from jumping on him.

It was so bizarre to witness her behaving this way, she was always so cool and put together that this seemed like a completely different person.

It didn't take long for security to show up. They promptly pulled Jani away from Sasha and carried her out the room.

She yelled obscenities the whole time and her yells slowly faded as she was carried farther down the driveway to her car.

Sasha and I stood staring at each other in disbelief.

He motioned towards me, but I was too disgusted to be near him, so I turned and walked out of the room holding Sadie close to me.

15

Sasha followed me around the estate the rest of the week.

I did my best to avoid him but he kept begging to let him explain the situation between he and Jani. But, I was too exhausted with his infidelities to entertain another one of his conquests.

Needing some privacy, I locked myself in my dressing room rereading Craig's message to meet with him in London at the Death of Love concert.

What did I have to lose? I was in an unhappy marriage that was not likely to last much longer. So, I texted him back.

Sam: Hey sorry for not responding sooner. I'd love to see you at the show in London.

My heart pounded loudly after sending the text.

Within seconds my phone chimed.

It was Craig.

Craig: Cool! I was hoping you would. We are already here

doing interviews and promotions. I'll send you the details.

I sat on the floor clutching the phone to my chest wondering how my life would have been different if Craig and I had worked out.

He was always so in love with me. I doubted he would have humiliated me with other women like Sasha did.

I took a deep breath and readied myself.

It was time to leave Sasha.

I left my dressing room, went into my bedroom and put my diamond wedding ring in a small velvet box and set it on the night stand with a note that read goodbye.

I grabbed a small bag and filled it with my clothes and essentials from my bathroom. I needed to move quickly while Sasha was in his office.

I also needed to get Sadie. I wanted to take Sean with me but with me not being his birth mother it would be problematic legally.

Sadie's car seat was already in my SUV, so all I had to do was pack her things.

Her room was adjourned to mine so I was able to collect her bag and some baby food from her small pink refrigerator.

Thankfully, she stayed asleep as I crept down the stairs and by Sasha's office door.

I hurried down the corridor toward the garage.

I sighed an air of relief as I made it to my SUV and opened the back door to place Sadie into her carseat.

As soon as she was settled in, she awoke suddenly with fury in her eyes. I forgot how much she loath being in her carseat. I would always have to bribe her with ice cream and cookies just to keep quiet for a short ride.

But, at this moment I was not prepared and she threw

the biggest tantrum and began kicking, screaming, and wriggling from my grasp.

"Sadie! SHHHHHH! Sadie! Stop!"

It was too late.

The garage door raised open with Sasha's security guard on the other side. Then, Sasha ran through the door into the garage with Dijon close behind.

"What is going on?" Sasha yelled at the top of his throat.

I trembled as I continued trying to get Sadie to stay in her carseat as she fought me with all her might.

Sasha reached over me and picked up Sadie who was still kicking and hollering. He immediately handed her to Dijon.

He glanced at the packed bags and realized what I was up to.

"You are not taking my daughter." His eyes were cold and fixed on me in a way that sent a chill down my spine.

"She's my daughter! She belongs to me!" I cried out as the tears streamed down my cheeks.

"If you want to go. Go. But, you are not dragging my daughter away from her home." Sasha blocked me at the car door.

I tried to push past him toward Dijon.

"Dijon, take Sadie back inside." He called out.

Dijon did as ordered and whisked Sadie still crying into the house and closed the door.

The security guard stood steady in the garage opening. I realized I had to leave without my Sadie.

"She's my baby." I tried pleading with Sasha, but he was unmoved as his stare became colder.

"She's my baby, too." He placed his hands on my shoulders trying to keep his composure.

"You go wherever you want and once you become settled in a suitable home, we can discuss you seeing

Sadie." He held the car door open for me to enter then slammed it shut.

My chest felt empty as if he'd ripped my heart out.

The guard stepped aside as I started the car and drove down the long driveway and into the unknown.

Part VI: Lexi

16

'I Was Apart of Sasha's Harem'

Casey graced the front of the online gossip blog with the headline. I downloaded every online publication covering the scandal.

It was absurd to see this and have her mention me as some type of madam who was working for Sasha to keep her here.

A knot tightened in my abdomen as I combed through the articles rereading and studying each section carefully as if the interpretation would somehow change.

I had not left the house since my affair with Sasha became public.

I kept the blinds shut and didn't even go into the backyard since the neighbors' homes were so close they could easily peer into the backyard.

Every so often I looked out the front window, and there were always a few diehard paparazzi camped outside waiting for me to emerge.

My cellphone rang constantly with so-called friends from back home wanting the scoop. The only time I answered was when it was my mom. My father, likely disappointed in my lifestyle choices, refused to speak to me.

Searching my name online and reading all the negative comments about me being a 'bad friend to Sam' 'backstabber' 'home wrecker' and worst of all 'madam' began to take its toll on my mental health, but I obsessively continued reading them anyway.

My dream career as a songwriter was slowly becoming a nightmare that I could not wake from.

I thought being with Sasha would elevate me in my career, but now it seemed a wasted effort. And, the funny part is Sam was never a good friend to me, we both used each other. She would have done the same thing as me if she were in my shoes.

Everyone making her out to be some defenseless, righteous matriarch would be in shock if they really knew her and how she climbed her way into rock star royalty.

My cellphone rang and I answered immediately when I saw my mom's picture on the caller id. She was the only person I could talk to. And, I really needed someone to talk to.

"Hey, mom."

"Oh, baby. You sound horrible. Are you still obsessing over those silly news articles?"

"I can't help it."

"You have to stay strong, Lexi."

There was a silence as I contemplated how one could stay strong in this situation.

"Well, the reason I'm calling is your cousin Jason who just passed the bar exam said that you have some rights and can sue this Casey girl and the news outlet for defamation. And, since you didn't sign a non-disclosure agreement with Sasha, you can be compensated for speaking your side of the scandal."

"Mom. I really can't deal with this right now." My head was throbbing at the thought of pursuing legal action.

"You're gonna have to deal with it. You made the decision to be with this MARRIED man, so now you need to make some moves to ensure you will be okay. This has ruined your reputation and possibly your songwriting career."

Hearing this out loud suddenly made it seem real.

"Look, now, don't get angry with me, but a lady you were working with named Veronica called me because you were avoiding her calls and said you need to get in front of this. She also said you could make millions with a book deal and interviews."

"She called you!" The audacity of Veronica. "Mom! She's the one who leaked the story!"

"Oh, you don't know that for sure. But, honey this man has taken advantage of you. You are the victim here. He has tons of money and he will be just fine. You need to start putting your needs first and if this agent Veronica can help you, let her."

I realized it was no point debating this with my mom and at this point my stomach was turning with disgust at the thought of Veronica 'helping me' and I wanted the conversation to end.

"I hear you, Ma. It's been a stressful few days, so let me sleep on it before I make a final decision."

"Okay, sweetheart. You know I love you and just want the best for you."

"I know mom. And, I love you too."

After hanging up with my mom, I was more confused and uncertain about what to do and how my future would look.

I got a notification of another media posting of the scandal.

I needed to shut down my laptop and focus on something else.

My finger hovered over the power off button, but my curiosity grew as the notification icon set on the screen as if begging me to read it.

I inhaled deeply, this one could be different.

I moved my finger away from the power off button and clicked on the notification.

17

"Veronica! Give us a comment!"

"Are you representing Lexi!"

"What does she have to say to her former best friend!"

The paparazzi surrounded Veronica as she ascended the stairs towards the door with a satisfied smile on her face.

As I watched from the window she didn't seem to mind the attention as she came prepared with large black designer sunglasses to block the camera flashes.

Her curly hair had grown out just past her ears and was dyed a dark pink. She wore a dark purple suit jacket with black faux leather pants.

I decided it would not hurt to take my mother's advice and meet with her. I had not heard anything from Sasha so I assumed he abandoned me and left me to fend for myself.

I hid from the paparazzi behind the door as I opened it to allow Veronica to slip through into the foyer.

"Oh you poor thing!" She wrapped her arms around my neck and held me tight. "How are you holding up being locked away in this so-called love nest?"

She was pushing for confirmation of this being Sasha's harem. I was on to her manipulations by now and decided to ignore the question.

"My mom convinced me to meet with you about how I should move forward." I pulled away from her grasp.

"Of course." She brushed past me into the living room and made herself comfortable on the couch.

"You keep it very clean here considering the circumstances." She looked around examining the room.

"Well, I haven't had much time for anything else these days."

I was still annoyed with her being here since I knew she was the one who cause this drama in the first place.

She pulled a folder from her purse and opened it to what looked like a contract and some hand-written notes on yellow post its on top.

"With you being a former roommate of Sasha's wife, the most notable talk shows and interviewers are willing to pay top dollar for your side of the story. And, with you not having a nondisclosure agreement you are in the perfect position to fully benefit from this. I don't know how you pulled that off because Casey and all of his former girlfriends signed one. I even tried to work with his former nanny, Lily, but she has an ironclad NDA, plus he and Sam have a restraining order against her."

"Wait, you're working with Casey?" I did not realize just how low she would go.

"I spoke with her and tried to help her but the cease and desist letters from Sasha's lawyers are putting her story on pause, possibly inevitably." She shuffled through the papers in the folder and pulled out one with a list of publishing houses.

"I have a list of publishers who are going to commit to a

very nice advance and book deal. Now, I'm also working with a few producers who would like to do a documentary on Sasha and the rock and roll industry in regards to how women have been taken advantage of."

"What ever happened to the South African singer that I was supposed to work with?" My question startled her as she looked up.

"That will still happen, but this is more important." She moved her attention back to the papers.

I just sat quietly in the arm chair thinking everything over.

Do I want to do this? It strangely felt like a betrayal of Sasha.

Did he really violate me or anyone? Even with moving Casey in here, I didn't feel in my heart that his life deserved to be ruined because of it.

Veronica noticed my hesitation and moved closer towards me, leaning in with a soft, caring expression constructed on her face. She was good, but I was not fooled.

"Look. Let's talk real here. Your career in this industry is likely at a dead end at this point. You need to take action to ensure you will not end up living in your mother's basement because you missed out on this opportunity for something you thought was love with a man who did not choose to marry you, but decided to marry your pretty, skinny, white friend instead."

She cleared her throat.

"How many times have women like you and I been overlooked in this industry. Because I can assure you that Sasha choosing to marry her and putting her in the spotlight, yet keeping you in the shadows was to preserve his image. I mean, where is he? Has he contacted you? I bet not. He is banking on the fact that you are under his control and would not dare call him out on his crap. I understand you more than you think, Lexi. I have been where you are and have witnessed countless other women be devalued like this. You deserve better."

As much as I hated her, the words she spoke were real. I recalled all the times I was overlooked and taken advantage of while Sam just glided right up the ladder without breaking a sweat.

But, she oddly seemed to take this whole thing against Sasha very personally.

Veronica laid the contract on the coffee table.

"This is a contract that will allow me to represent you as your agent. Lexi, I will ensure that you will be a very wealthy woman after all of this. I will excuse myself to the powder room and give you a moment to look over the contract."

She walked into the small toilet at the base of the staircase.

I picked up the contract and began reading over it when suddenly I saw a ladder being lowered over the side of the stone wall that separated the back yard from the neighbor's.

Thinking it was one of the paparazzi trying to sneak a picture of me with Veronica, I quickly grabbed my cellphone to call the police. Then, I noticed it was Sasha struggling in a tight pair of dark blue jeans to climb over the wall and onto the ladder.

The neighbor's husband was trying to assist him by holding onto his waist, but he also seemed to struggle with Sasha being much larger than my neighbor's very slim frame. But, somehow they managed it and Sasha made his way down the ladder and marched right up to the glass sliding door.

"Is she here?" He mimed from the other side of the glass

making sure Veronica could not hear him.

Stunned I just nodded my head and pointed at the powder room door.

As soon as Veronica opened the door Sasha scurried behind a tall bush and he waved for the neighbor to duck behind the wall. But, the ladder was still visible.

"So, were you able to look it over?" She stood in front of me with her arms crossed.

I stood frozen, still holding the contract.

"I know this is a lot to take in, but we need to move quickly and get ahead of this."

The only thing I needed now was for her to leave.

"You're right. This is a lot to take in. Give me some time to think everything over."

Her eyes widened.

"Let's talk about this. What is concerning you about taking this next step in your career?"

"Veronica, right now I just need to clear my head. I'm not making a decision today. How about I think it over tonight and tomorrow we move forward with whatever decision I make?"

Her expression became stern and cold.

"Don't ruin your future, Lexi. This is all you have left."

Her words stung, but I had to talk to Sasha.

"I will call you first thing in the morning."

She sighed deeply and grabbed her large expensive designer purse from the couch, brushed past me and walked out the door into the paparazzi frenzy.

"What did you two talk about?" One called out.

"Is she going to make a statement?" Another shoved a microphone in her face.

Relieved she didn't notice the ladder, I ran to the sliding door to let Sasha in.

As soon as the door slid open he wrapped me in his

arms and kissed me.

I almost cried as all the emotions rushed inside of me all at once.

"We don't have much time. Herb next door owes me a favor and is going to sneak us out of here. Grab a small bag and I'll have my assistant gather your things later."

I ran up the stairs and packed a small overnight bag. My heart raced with excitement.

I knew he would not abandon me.

I knew he loved me.

18

My stomach jumped as the helicopter turned sharply over the Scottish Highland islands.

Sasha kept his composure while I struggled to keep my nausea down from the dips and turns of the helicopter flight.

"Look down, see how beautiful the islands are from up here" Sasha noticed my discomfort and tried his best to distract me.

He was right. The view of the islands were magnificent.

The greenery of the large cliffs and the water sparkled in the sunlight.

I never thought a place could look so surreal as this.

Sasha kept a house here near the distillery that makes his scotch whiskey. The locals knew and respected him so he felt safe here from the paparazzi and the media.

"I was born on that island where we are about to land." He peered out the small window.

"I thought you were English." I was shocked to hear that he was born here.

"Well, my father is English but my mother is Scottish

and from this island. We moved with my father to England when I was a boy. But, I spent every summer here with my grandparents. When my mother passed she left me the family land. That's why I decided to start a whiskey brand here to honor my mother's heritage."

It was interesting hearing this because Sasha rarely discussed his childhood.

I was relieved when we finally landed onto the helipad.

An escort dressed in black and wearing ear muffs opened the door while the blades were still going and Sasha jumped out without hesitation.

The swirling blades were so loud I set back, but the escort expertly held my head down guiding me out and away from the helipad.

The smell of salt water filled my nostrils as soon as we were clear of the helicopter.

There was a black SUV parked in front of the large airplane hanger and the driver was holding the back door open for us.

As soon as we were settled inside the driver quickly drove onto a small paved road that led up a steep hill overlooking the sea.

The drop to the water became higher as we ascended further up the hill.

After 10 minutes, we came to a large stone house overlooking the cliff to the water.

Sasha climbed out of the SUV, took a deep inhale, and stretched out his arms.

"Welcome to the land of my forefathers."

As we approached the edge of the steep cliff, I tried my best to admire the beautiful lush landscape in spite of us standing at such a high elevation over the large rocks being beaten by the large waves crashing in.

I could barely pay attention to Sasha as he talked about his childhood memories in the Scottish Highland islands.

The strong wind slung my braids into my face so strong that it stung as each strand slapped across my cheeks.

I stood very still trying to keep my composure while Sasha pointed at different places and explained their significance. Then, a powerful gush of wind hit me so hard I lost my balance.

"Gotcha! Be careful now!" He held me tightly to keep me from falling.

I'm sure he felt my heart racing, so he suggested we take a stroll away from the cliff's edge.

As we walked along a path in the meadows, I was able to appreciate the scenic beauty of the island.

A hare bounced just past us and disappeared into the tall grass dotted with small colorful flowers that swayed gently in the breeze.

Birds sang and chirped as they flew by with one clutching a small fish in its beak.

After the drama I was facing back in London, this was a much needed escape.

A small truck drove up the dirt path and the driver waved in our direction.

"Oh! Here is Willis. We are going to the distillery to taste a new whiskey I'm launching later this year."

We climbed into the small truck and went down the hillside to a large warehouse with three smaller stone outbuildings around it.

"This is the distillery. You can smell the peat burning from a mile away."

He was right, the smell of burning soil grew heavier as we approached the distillery.

An older man walked with an excited pep in his step

from one of the smaller outbuildings.

"Hallow!" He waved and greeted us in a deep Scottish accent.

"We havre everything prepared for ye visit. Hallow young lady. How're you enjoy'n Skye so far?"

"I love it here." I felt giddy at his kindness and excitement to greet us.

"Oh! Is that a Southern accent I hear?" He nodded his head as if he discovered a secret.

"Yes. I'm from Atlanta, Georgia."

"I suspected as much. Well, ye will definitely enjoy yer self in the nature here."

"Yes. Thank you."

He shook Sasha's hand and led us into the large stone warehouse.

"Now, Mr. Sasha is already very familiar with how the whisky is processed but wer'll still take a tour so that ye can learn how our magical spirit is made. So, first wer'll show ye where that wonderful peat smoked filled air is coming from."

After an extensive tour of the distillery, our guide brought us to a large open space filled with huge oak barrels.

"Here ye will have yer tasting." The guide extended his arm toward a small hightop table with two small oval shaped sniffer glasses and five different bottles of Scottish whiskey.

Sasha took my hand in his and led me to the table. He pulled out my chair so that I could climb in and he sat in the chair next to me.

"I am going to have you try some of the best whiskey in the Highlands." He picked up a bottle with a label that read 31 years.

"It is always best to start with the oldest whiskey first

in a tasting because it's the smoothest and most delicate on the palate. If you look here you will see the years it spent in the barrel, which is 31 years, and the type of barrel it was in. The most common type are American Bourbon oak barrels because they are more readily available. But, this was aged in Oloroso Sherry casts coming from Andalusia in southern Spain. You can see the barrel's origin on the label here."

He poured a small amount in the glass, I could smell spicy dried fruit right away.

I followed his lead and sniffed the whiskey, then I took a sip.

The smooth liquid felt like silk coating the inside of my mouth. It lingered there and I could feel the silkiness slowly going down and coating my throat.

"I've never experienced anything like this before." I could not believe the sensations happening all at once in my mouth.

"I'm glad to hear that. This is from my barrels for my new line of whiskey. This bottle will retail for over 500 US dollars."

"Seriously, people pay this much."

"Oh, yes. You my dear are drinking some of the finest Scottish whiskey ever made."

I was delightfully lightheaded after spending the day drinking expensive whiskey and walking around town with Sasha.

After our tasting, he took the bottle and we went to a cozy local pub as it began to rain and set in a secluded corner. No one bothered us as we kissed, drank, and ate many local Scottish delicacies.

I didn't want this day to ever end, but deep down there was a slight pain of knowing that this would likely be our last night together.

Since the rain finally calmed, Sasha decided it was best to walk the ten minutes to his home and enjoy the night sky.

The moon and stars glowed so bright it illuminated the landscape and there was barely a need for lampposts.

I took in deep breaths of the clean, crisp air and walked quietly hand in hand with him.

He did not speak the whole way. It was as if he felt the same pain of this being our lasts moments.

With his stone house in view, he held my hand tighter the closer we moved towards it.

When we reached his front, he wiped away a tear from his cheek and led me through the small wooded door.

"How about you go upstairs and put on your pajamas while I get a fire started in the living room."

I nodded my head and went up the narrow wooden staircase to the small bedroom.

After I changed into a silk pink neglige and robe, I made my way back down the stairs.

Sasha sat in front of the stone fireplace on an old bear skinned rug that once belonged to his grandfather.

The flames from the fireplace lit and warmed the whole house.

He laid a charcuterie tray out on the coffee table behind him with local cheeses, fruit, and sliced meats.

His skin glowed in the light as he took a sip of red wine while staring in a trance into the fire.

I stood behind him and ran my fingers through his hair. He looked up at me and we just stared into each others' eyes.

I moved to face him then slowly lowered myself and straddled his lap.

He became erect as I pressed myself against him.

He wrapped his arms around me and kissed my chest, then my neck, and he stared deep into my eyes before kissing my lips.

He pulled my braids forcing my head backwards as he buried his face in my chest. Opening my robe and revealing my breasts, he wrapped his mouth around one and caressed my nipple with the tip of his tongue.

"You are so beautiful."

A gasp of pleasure escaped my mouth.

I cradled his face in my hands and kissed him.

He pulled down the front of his pants, then pushed himself inside of me.

I tried to take as much of him inside of me as I could.

As I moved up and down my robe became hot on my back from the heat that radiated from the fireplace. It became so hot that it slightly singed my skin with every motion I made.

I didn't care about the discomfort of the heat, I wanted him so badly in that moment, I would have endured every pain.

His head became heavy as he let out his usual moan of pleasure when he was near orgasm.

I needed to remember every smell, every touch, every taste because this night was likely our last night.

Tears welled in my eyes and my jaw trembled.

I could no longer hold back the grief of losing him. A cry escape my mouth and he held me tighter, kissing the tears that streamed down my face.

The staleness of whiskey from his warm breath filled my nostrils as he rocked back and forth beneath me.

His body stiffened suddenly and he held me firmly in his embrace. His manhood pulsated inside of me as his warmth filled inside of me.

"I love you. I love so much." His heavy voice cracked

with emotion and exhaustion.

"I love you, too."

He wiped the tears from my cheeks with both hands and brought my face to his. Our eyes only an inch apart, he stared directly into mine as if in search of something.

Letting out a deep sigh, he set back against the coffee table.

I slid from his lap and sat next to him waiting for him to say something.

He turned and looked down at me.

"Tomorrow my lawyers will come here and ask you to sign a nondisclosure agreement." He paused to study my reaction.

"I want you to listen to me very carefully. I have a trust that is worth hundreds of millions of dollars and I told them to compensate you. When they pressure you to sign, you ask for what you want and get every penny that you can. They will fight you, but you are in the position of power. No one can force you to sign, but if you do decide to sign I want to know that you will be in a good place and secure financially. Demand them to give you what you want."

I set there and just stared back at him unable to utter a word.

"Promise me that you will not leave that meeting empty handed."

"I promise."

He leaned down and tenderly kissed my forehead.

Sasha left the house early the next morning and prepared me for the meeting with his lawyers. The small living room was cold and sad in his absence.

I sat on the couch with an emptiness in my chest as if my heart had left with him.

My thoughts were interrupted with a loud authoritative knock on the front door.

I opened the door to an older man and a middle-aged woman both dressed in dark suits with white button up shirts. They walked past me and sat at the wooded table in the kitchen that was just across from the living room.

I sat across from them as the man opened his briefcase and pulled out a contract of about 30 pages then plopped it in front of me with a smug expression.

He laid a black fountain pen on top of the stack of papers.

"I've highlighted the areas that you need to sign and initial. If you have any questions feel free to ask them."

We all sat in an awkward silence for a movement as I stared at the contract.

I took a deep breath and looked up at them.

He stared back at me with stern intimidation.

I swallowed then held my head high.

"I want five million dollars."

Part VII: Sam

19

"Here is the keycard to your room miss."

The man at the boutique hotel guest check-in desk cleared his throat and could only hold eye contact for a second before looking down at his desktop computer.

The news of my philandering husband was all over the media and being in Worthing not far from the estate, everyone knew who I was.

Well, at least he gave me the largest room on the top floor with a view of the sea.

I was tired and desperately needed a place to sleep and plan my next steps.

When I exited the elevator onto my floor, two women wearing hotel uniforms were whispering to each other.

As I made my way down the hall I noticed they were standing just outside my door.

One of the women noticed me approaching them and tapped the other one on the arm. They both stared at me then nodded with a greeting smile.

"Enjoy your stay!" One called out as they moved huddled together down the hallway.

I dropped my duffle bag by the bed and opened the sliding doors to the viewing balcony.

The sun was out and the sea was calm.

What was I going to do? I didn't know where to start.

I wanted to be with my daughter and little Sean will think that I abandoned him.

My cellphone chimed.

It was a text from Craig.

Craig: Hey. How are you holding up?

Sam: I left Sasha, but he blocked me from taking Sadie with me.

Then my cellphone rang, it was Craig.

"Hey." My voice was strained and exhausted.

"That asshole. How dare he separate you from your child. Where are you?"

"I'm at a hotel in Worthing. Everyone knows. I'm so humiliated." My voice cracked as tears swelled then rolled down my cheeks.

"Hey, I'm here for you. Tomorrow morning I have to meet with the promoters and do some interviews for the show. Drive to London tomorrow afternoon and you can stay with me. You should not be alone right now with everything you've been through."

"Okay. I will drive up there tomorrow."

"Text me when you leave the hotel and I will make sure to be here. Now, try to get some rest. I will take care of you, Sam."

"Thank you. I really needed to hear that."

I sat my cellphone on the small table and felt relief that everything would be okay.

I have Craig, now.

He would protect me and make everything better.

Craig laid on his back with his arm wrapped around me allowing my head to rest on his shoulder.

His breathing was steady as his chest lifted with each deep inhale and letting out a soft snore when he exhaled.

I was in and out of sleep throughout the night. It was surreal making love to him again. I remembered his smell and his smooth skin, but it still felt so foreign to me.

The thought of Sasha and the life I was leaving brought tears to my eyes, but I tried to hold them back.

Craig was so patient with me.

My life was a circus now and I needed him.

I glanced at the red neon time on the digital clock on the hotel nightstand.

4:16 AM.

My body was so tired but my brain was too active to fall back to sleep. I wished the time would move faster as I tried to stay as still as possible to avoid disturbing Craig.

"Can't sleep" Craig let out a yarn.

"I just have a lot on my mind. I didn't want to wake you."

"You can wake me whenever you like." He turned onto his side and kissed my brow.

His erection pressed against my stomach.

I could tell he wanted to make love again. A part of me wanted to, but I it still felt so unfamiliar being intimate with him.

His hand moved over my bottom and he slid a finger inside of me.

"Oh, you're so wet." His moist lips wrapped around mine.

He rolled on top of me and pushed himself inside of me, then slowly moving his hips back and forth pushing himself in deeper.

I laid still trying to be in the moment but my mind wondered and a part of me wanted him to climax quickly.

I ran my hands over his slightly textured skin and recalled how smooth and soft Sasha's skin was when we made love.

It was so hard to stop thinking about Sasha.

"Hey, you okay?" Craig squinted his eyes at me, studying my face.

"Yeah. I just didn't sleep well."

"I can stop if you want." He started to climb out of the bed.

"No. I want you to make love to me. I missed you." I felt bad for not being present with him.

I had to remember that he was here for me and I really wanted this to work out between us.

"Are you sure?"

I pushed him onto his back and realized he went soft.

He laid his head on the pillow as I put my mouth over his manhood and immediately it began to stiffen.

His body relaxed and he placed his hand on my cheek.

He looked so happy and at peace with a smirk at the corner of his mouth.

"I'm so happy you're here."

I just smiled back as he stared into my eyes.

"I love you."

The words flowed out of him so effortlessly, leaving me in shock.

"Was that too soon?" He looked concerned as I sat up, frozen.

"No! I just wasn't expecting it."

"Okay. So, you don't feel the same?" He looked away.

"I do." My voice cracked. "It's just been a lot going on."

He looked down and sighed.

"Craig, I love you. Just understand that I had to leave my daughter behind and everything is crazy right now."

He nodded still looking down.

I leaned in and kissed him for reassurance.

"I understand, Sam."

He wrapped his arms around me and pulled me into his chest.

I glance at the clock and it was 6:03 AM.

"Is it too early to order breakfast?" My stomach growled and I remembered not eating any dinner the night before.

"I'm sure the kitchen is open. Let's see what they have."

Craig grabbed the menu from behind the lamp and looked over the breakfast options.

"How about we order a stack of pancakes, omelets, sausage, and mimosas?"

"Yes." I kissed his cheek as he called for room service.

The sun was just coming up and the light began to fill the room. I opened the curtains and stared at the concrete roof of the hotel's garage. Cars raced down the expressway in the background and a few other midsized hotels set in the distance.

It wasn't the type of view I had become accustomed to.

I closed the shear curtains and set at the small table by the television stand.

Craig went into the toilet after ordering room service.

I sat there in silence looking around the small hotel room and my eyes settled on my small duffle bag with few clothes in it.

Craig came out of the toilet, humming a tune to himself.

"It's chilly in here. You can wear my hoodie." He took a large grey hoodie from his suitcase and pulled it over my head. The hard cotton fibers of the hoodie felt rough on my skin.

He walked over to the window and opened the shear

curtains revealing the garage and now congested traffic.

He took a deep inhale.

"I think it's going to be a good day."

20

The attorney who helped negotiate my prenup with Sasha text me to meet him in his office later that day.

I drove to the large glass office building in Central London. After valeting I rushed into the building to avoid being recognized.

Thankfully his office was on the 6th floor so I didn't need to stay on the elevator long.

Most of the walls were glass with large floor to ceiling windows allowing the sun to shine in and fill up the whole office suite.

I spotted my attorney, David, in his glass office sitting at his desk. He rested his chin on his hand while staring at a document.

I knocked on the door, he looked up and waved me to enter.

"Good morning, Sam." His voice was monotone.

"Good morning, David."

He laid down the papers and stared at me with an annoyed expression as I settled into a chair facing him.

Suddenly, I felt nervous that I did something wrong.

He cleared his throat and set back in his leather chair.

"I just received information that you are staying with a man named Craig at a hotel. Is this true?"

Puzzled, I nodded.

"Well, there is an infidelity clause in your prenuptial agreement. By violating your prenup, you do not get any spousal support and you have forfeited your annuity."

My throat became dry and my voice cracked.

"Wait. What do you mean?"

"You should have called me before speaking to or seeing anyone. I would have advised you of your next steps."

"But, we're separated. And, being in a hotel room with a man does not prove infidelity." My heart began to race.

"You are still legally married and the hotel staff person who delivered your room service confirmed to your husband's lawyers that you and this Craig appeared to have had sexual relations."

David stared blankly at me waiting for my response.

"So, what do I do?" My cheeks warmed as my eyes strained as I looked over the desk at David.

"Well, the only thing you can do at this point is get an inexpensive divorce and work with your husband on a custody agreement. Or, you can try to work things out and chose to stay married."

"This is not right? Can we sue? The annuity belongs to me. He cheated on me throughout our marriage and it's all over the media about his haram he kept in London."

"Technically, the annuity is owned by Sasha along with all of the other assets which is in a trust. You cannot sue him for anything no matter how he behaved. And, with the non-disclosure agreement you signed, you can't even sue the trust but you can work out a deal through them internally."

Tension began to build up in my head. I could not believe what was happening right now.

He glanced at me with pity.

"Look, if you really want to go through with this divorce and see no way of working this out, try talking to Sasha. Don't yell, threaten, or accuse him of anything. Just play on his sympathies. I do not think he is the type to just leave you with nothing."

We sat there in an awkward silence as I stared at the prenup hoping there was a loophole.

"Um, I have another meeting in a few minutes. So, I suggest you take some time to think things over, then call my assistant with your next steps."

He stood up, walked around his desk and held the glass door open for my dismissal.

Stunned at his brashness, I walked defeated out of his office.

Everyone in the office avoided eye contact with me as if they all knew of my mistake.

The elevator seemed to take forever to come, leaving me standing alone in the office entryway trying my best not to cry.

21

"Hey, everything is going to be fine. I will take care of you."

Craig reassured me over the phone.

I didn't know where else to go, so I just went back to the hotel room.

Craig was about to go into a radio interview with the band to promote their concert.

"The interview is about to begin. Just order some food and get some rest, you've had a stressful day. When I get back, I'll take you out shopping for some new clothes."

"Okay."

I hung up the phone feeling helpless.

The last thing I could do right now was rest. My mind ran through all of the scenarios that would have put me in a better position.

David was right, I should have called him with my plans before leaving my home and my daughter.

I needed to talk to someone who could fix this.

I decided to call my psychic, Spring. I had not spoken to her in a few months, yet was still paying the $1000 each month.

I sent her a text if she had any openings today for a reading. She text back immediately that she would call me in 20 minutes.

I was desperate for her guidance. I could not stand the uncertainty of everything that was happening.

The annuity I received from Sasha was my safety net and with that gone I didn't know how I would survive. I left all of my jewels, clothes, and Sasha will eventually tow my car away from the hotel.

He handled all of the finances so I didn't own anything outside of him.

I heard my cellphone and picked it up on the first ring.

"Spring, thank you so much for calling me."

"Of course, Sam. I have been following everything in the media. How are you holding up?"

"I'm not doing so good right now." My voice trembled and then I just burst into tears.

"Oh no! Tell me everything, my love."

I told her about how I had to leave Sadie behind, being with Craig and losing my annuity because of it.

"Wow. That is a lot you went through, Sam. Let me speak with spirit and pull some tarot."

There was a long pause. I could only hear the sound of cards shuffling as I gripped my cellphone so firm my hands were becoming numb.

"I see here that you have lost a lot and will have some financial difficulties. Craig will be faithful to you and love you dearly, but it will not be enough for you. You will soon see that the two of you are not compatible." She took a deep breath. "Right now you are at a crossroads and the choices you make at this point cannot be reversed. Sasha does love you very much, yet he can love many at once. It is not that he is being cruel, it is just the way he loves. Not everyone loves the same."

"But, it's humiliating. Is it wrong to want a faithful husband." I couldn't understand how someone can love several people at the same time.

"It is not wrong to want this. But, you need to remember why you wanted him in the first place. Before you make a final decision on the path you take, go back to the beginning of this journey. What was your goal? I am sure that it was not to just have a faithful husband because you could have had that with DJ back in Georgia. You wanted something more for yourself and you got everything you wanted. Finally, you grasped a shooting star, now you can either fly with it or get left in its dust."

I appreciated Spring's words of wisdom, but I did not feel any better nor had any idea of what I should do next.

"Oh no! Not you again!"

Joe stood before me with his grey hair a lot thinner since the last time I saw him when he managed Fred's band. Apparently, he was now managing Death of Love.

I followed Craig in through the large wooden doors of an old church that was converted into a performance venue.

I ignored Joe and grabbed Craig's hand as we continued into the empty auditorium.

"Hey, have a seat here while I meet with the rest of the band in the dressing room."

I settled onto a stool at an empty bar and watched Joe follow Craig through the backstage door. I knew he was going to say something bad about me and do his best to break us up.

I looked around the large space and sat patiently at the bar for Craig to return.

About 30 minutes later I heard Joe's voice echoing through the room.

"She ruined that man's career. He was going places, but would not listen to me about her. Now, look at him. That woman is trouble. Get out while you can, man."

Craig walked back into the auditorium with Joe still following behind him.

He kissed my check and sat on the stool next to me.

Joe rolled his eyes and went outside into the parking lot.

"Is everything okay?" I placed my hand on Craig's thigh.

"Yeah, we're just waiting for Johnny to show up so we can rehearse." He squeezed my hand.

"SAM! Good to see you!"

Luzar emerged from the backstage doorway with a grin so wide that the fillers in his face protruded forward.

He walked cockily behind the bar and rummaged through the small beverage fridge to retrieve a bottle of water.

Craig and I gave each other a look of annoyance at Luzar's presence.

He walked back around the bar and wrapped his arms around me. Then, kissed my cheek.

"It's good to see you two love birds back together. Maybe the three of us can have some fun later." Luzar glanced down at my cleavage.

"That's enough Luzar." Craig grabbed his arm pulled him away from me.

"Chill man. I'm just being friendly." Luzar chuckled and went back to the backstage area.

"This band is the only reason I tolerate him." Craig rolled his eyes.

I heard the entrance door open and Joe speaking loudly.

"Finally! Hey guys, Johnny's here! Let's get this rehearsal started!" Joe started clapping his hands to get everyone's attention.

Johnny entered the room and following right behind him was Lexi.

My skin warmed and turned red as if my blood was boiling at the sight of her.

She walked towards the bar and stopped mid-step when she locked eyes with me.

I don't know what came over me, but I leap from the barstool and lunged at her with full force.

Part VIII: Lexi

22

I froze as Sam lunged towards me with her long auburn hair flying wildly on her head.

She wrapped her hands around my throat and began choking me while screaming incoherently.

I started shoving her in the face to free myself but her grasp was too firm.

Johnny and Craig jumped between us and did their best to pull us apart. She dug her nails so deep into my skin that she scraped my neck raw when Johnny finally pulled her away.

I gasped for air as she flailed her arms and legs while Craig held her.

"That bitch! She slept with my husband! You ruined my fucking life!"

Joe stood aside with a bewildered smile as he watched the altercation.

Luzar and Zach ran through the backstage door and stood next to Joe.

"Hey, are you okay?" Johnny looked over the scratches on my neck.

My throat was sore so all I could do was nod.

Sam cried into Craigs chest as he held her tightly.

Johnny escorted me to the backstage area so I could hide out in the band's dressing room.

I went to the mirror to check my throat and saw long red welts with beads of blood forming on top.

My hands were still trembling as I fumbled through a cabinet looking for a first aide kit.

This was the last place I thought I would see her.

I understood her anger towards me but I never thought she would attack me like that.

I grabbed the first aide kit from the back of the cabinet and found some rubbing alcohol wipes.

"Hey, Craig is taking Sam back to the hotel. Come to the bar, we found where they're stashing the liquor."

I missed standing side stage while watching the band perform.

The all three nights at the venue was sold out and the first night they put on a really good show.

I danced the whole time and Johnny even ran over to kiss me between one of their songs.

I missed him so much.

After the show the band had a meet and greet at a bar area backstage for fans who won raffles or paid for vip tickets.

The band was so excited to see so many people who paid the vip to hang out with them after the show. There were at least 100 fans that filled up the small space.

Instead of having everyone stand in a line for autographs, they set up an after show party where everyone enjoyed free drinks and took pictures.

I sat at the bar and watched the guys mingle with their fans and posed for pictures. A few ruder fans took pictures of me and gawked at the audacity of me being there.

I just did my best to ignore them.

Johnny was especially excited. He was afraid they were forgotten in the industry, but to have so many people in another country here, gave them hope for the future.

Craig left after an hour to meet up with Sam.

After three hours of partying backstage, the venue had to close so everyone who wanted to continue partying met up at a nearby after-hours lounge.

I was already tipsy from the three drinks at the afterparty, I really did not need any more.

When we got out of the cab to go inside the lounge, a few paparazzi flashed their cameras at us and one asked Johnny what if felt like to date a home wrecker.

We ignored them and continued walking into the club.

The atmosphere was more chill and calm than backstage at the venue. About 50 people from the after show party were there including a few crew members.

Luzar and Zach went directly to two blonde women they met backstage who were now sitting at the bar.

Johnny and I settled on a long L-shaped couch in the back corner with a few executives and crew members joining us.

He rested his arm around my shoulders and playfully nibbled my earlobe.

"So, everyone is saying you likely got a ton of money to sign a nondisclosure." He whispered in my ear.

"I can't discuss anything." I sat up and took a sip of my drink.

I recalled the lawyers saying that revealing the amount I received would be a breach of the contract. I could be sued and have to return the 5 million dollars.

I loved Johnny very much, but I was not going to lose

millions of dollars after everything I went through with Sasha.

"Babe, that agent you had, Veronica, said in an interview that she had million dollar book deals and interviews lined up but you decided to sign a nondisclosure agreement. I know you did not do that without getting paid."

He lean towards me waiting for a reply.

"There's nothing to discuss." I turned away and stared into my drink.

He removed his arm from around my shoulders and sat back on the couch.

I wanted to avoid any further discussion, so I stood from the couch and walked to the restroom.

Three younger women were huddled together in front of a mirror over a pedestal sink. They became quiet when I walked in and watched me as I went into one of the stalls.

I could hear them whispering about me and felt so uncomfortable that I could not relieve myself.

They were still standing over the sink which was the only one in the restroom when I walked out the stall.

"Excuse me I need to wash my hands." They all stared at my reflection in the mirror as I stood behind them.

"Sure, go ahead." A brunette said in a perky English accent.

They stepped aside but I still had to brush past them to wash my hands.

They hovered over me and stared at me sizing me up.

"So, what is it about you that Sasha and Johnny like?" The raven haired one was speaking now.

I stayed quiet, pulled a paper towel from the dispenser, and walked out.

"Rude, bitch!" The other brunette called out.

I took a deep inhale and made my way back to Johnny.

He was talking to two girls with long straight black hair who were sitting on either side of him.

I approached them and Johnny looked up at me with a smirk.

"Ladies this is my girlfriend. Could one of you move over for her to sit?"

One of the girls moved over and rolled her eyes at me.

I set down and they continued talking.

"I like your braids." One of the girls reached over and pulled on one of my strands.

"Thanks." I pulled my hair from her hand.

"She was just giving you a complement." The other girl snapped.

"Ladies! We are having a fun night, let's get along." Johnny spread both arms over us to calm everyone.

"This is Lana and Tana. They work together in the adult film industry." He winked at me.

"We are the top performers in the adult film industry." Lana corrected him.

"Oh, excuse me. Top performer. I love your British accents. Say something dirty?"

Lana leaned in and whispered something into his ear.

"WOW! Seriously! I'm so down for that!"

I was annoyed with Johnny and ready to leave. I knew he was doing this because I wouldn't talk to him about Sasha and the money.

"So, what about Lexi? Would you do that to her?" Johnny pulled Lana closer to him.

"I would so do that to her. She's sexy and I like a girl with attitude." Lana smiled seductively at me.

"Sexy Lexi!" Tana yelled out.

I went from anger to uncomfortable as Tana started running her hand up my thigh and tugging at the hem of my miniskirt.

Johnny gave me a mischievous look.

"Let's have some fun tonight, babe."

I knew exactly what he meant and I really wasn't in the mood for it, but I wanted to make him happy and stop asking about the money, so I nodded.

"Let's go ladies!"

Johnny and I laid back on the bed while Lana and Tana made out with each other wearing only their panties.

They behaved as though they were in front of a camera. The way they poised their naked bodies, made sultry glances at us, and moaned on cue.

I could tell Johnny was not into this at all.

It was like watching a bad adult film.

"Do you want to join us?" Lana extended her hand to us.

Johnny and I looked at each other and just burst out laughing.

"Ladies, let's call it a night." Johnny stood from the bed and handed them their dresses.

"What?" Tana's eyes darted back and forth, puzzled about what was happening.

"It's been a long night and l just want to get some rest right now. I thought I had the energy for a foursome but I'm sorry ladies, I just can't do it tonight." Johnny waited for them to get dressed then held the hotel room door open for them.

They rolled their eyes and scoffed at him as they stomped through the door.

Johnny released his grip on the door handle and let it slam shut behind them.

"Thank goodness! I was not into them at all." I climbed onto my knees on the bed and began taking my shirt off.

"That was really bad. I mean for me to turn down a

foursome it has to be horrible."

Johnny climbed onto the bed and helped me pull my shirt over my head.

He pulled my skirt up over my hips and laid me back onto the bed.

I ran my hands through his hair and gently tugged at the ends. He always liked when I did this.

He sat up and removed his clothes then climbed back on top of me and kissed me.

"Now, this is what I like."

23

It was good being back in Los Angeles.

I missed the long sunny days and warm weather.

In London, days like this were few and far between.

Death of Love played for three nights in London and had two weeks off before going back overseas to tour Europe. Most of the shows were already sold out and they booked a few festivals out there as well.

Everyone was still living off of the high of the band's success in London.

With the sold out shows and merchandise sales, they netted over $100,000, which was split between the four of them and Joe. So, Jonny pocketed $20,000 in three days. I could only imagine what he will earn during the European tour.

But, I quickly remembered haw bad he was with money.

He enjoyed luxury and going out.

In London, he went shopping and ate at the most expensive restaurants.

I was worried he would end up spending most of his

money on tour and coming home with barely enough to cover the rent.

When we lived together before, he had no idea how the bills were getting paid because most of the time I was paying them. When he went on tour, he rarely sent money to me for the bills, I just had to figure out how to pay them.

"Hey, why don't we stop renting and just buy a place." Johnny said.

We sat on the couch that we had in our old apartment.

He and Zach were still roommates and shared a two bedroom and bath in an old house that was transformed into apartment units.

"I was thinking about buying a place." I revealed. "We just need to figure out where we want to live."

Johnny sat up and faced me.

"Well, how about our old neighborhood in Santa Monica. I know you got at least a few million from Sasha. We can get something right on the beach."

"Those houses are over 10 million dollars! We can't afford that!" I sat up staring back at him.

"Why not? Use the money you got from the NDA and with the band back together I can cover the rest."

He'd been trying so hard to figure out how much I received for signing the NDA. I wished I could trust him enough to tell him, but I could not risk it.

"We were barely getting by when we were renting that expensive house in that neighborhood before. We can't put ourselves in that situation again." I laid my hand on his trying to get him to reason with me.

"But, this time it's different. We would own the house instead of renting it." He pulled his hand away in protest.

I sat back on the couch and contemplated what he was saying. I knew he was not financially responsible enough to maintain the mortgage payments. And, I would be back to hustling and doing side gigs just to keep the lights on.

I could not go back to living that way. I had so many aspirations I wanted to pursue with my song writing and I planned on moving into producing music.

"Why don't we find something not so expensive. Maybe we don't have to be on the beach. It's just the two of us. Maybe we can get something for around 500,000 dollars or at the most a million dollars."

"Is that how much you got from Sasha?" He stared into my eyes searching for confirmation.

I sighed loudly and turned away from him.

"Lexi, why do you hide money from me. Like when I thought we were struggling and you had fifty thousand dollars in your bank account. We could have stayed in our house with that money."

"Johnny, we could not afford that house. We were barely able to pay the rent and buy food at the same time."

"We could have made it work." He turned me back around to face him.

"No, we couldn't. When you went on tour, you rarely paid your half of the bills. You are so irresponsible with money. And, this time I cannot carry you. I have dreams and plans too. It's not just about your career."

I stood up from the couch and went to the bedroom.

I sat on the edge of the bed and stared at my reflection in the mirror on top of the dresser.

I thought I could try again with Johnny, but I realized he will never change. The only reason he wanted to be with me was because he assumed I was getting a lot of money from Sasha.

I heard Zach and Johnny whispering in the living room.

I tiptoed to the door to listen.

"So, how much did she get from him?" Zach whispered.

"I don't know. She's being really dodgy about it."

"Maybe she didn't get anything."

"She's a money magnet. Trust me these rich people always pay off their side pieces to make sure they don't talk."

Furious, I threw my things into my suitcase and stormed out of the bedroom.

Zach's eyes widened and he looked down at Johnny.

"What are you doing?" Johnny jumped up from the couch and ran towards me.

"I'm done with you, Johnny." I continued to the front door.

"Wait, what?" He blocked me from opening the door.

"You will never change. This whole relationship has been about you trying to live a rock star lifestyle that you can't afford. I'm not going back to busting my ass to carry you." I tried to shove my way past him.

"Just calm down. Let's not forget you would not be where you are if I had not chosen you." Johnny's face turned red as his pointed his finger at me.

"Chose me! You were lucky to have me because your ass would have been homeless if I did not work and take care of your responsibilities. This time I'm putting myself first. Find someone else to live off of."

I shoved Johnny to the side and stormed out into the single driveway to the house.

Johnny followed me out yelling.

"YOU FUCKING GROUPIE BITCH! You are just another female spreading her legs for whoever will pay the highest price. Maybe you can find another friend's husband to sleep with."

I requested a ride share on my cellphone and waited at the end of the driveway.

The neighbors were looking through the windows and coming outside to witness the commotion.

"You were nothing without me. Now, look at you Ms. High and Mighty. You're so much better with all your hoe money. Well, you deserve it." He continued as I stood praying for the ride share to show up soon.

Finally, the driver pulled up staring confused at Johnny throwing a temper tantrum behind me.

I quickly climbed into the backseat.

"Is everything okay?" The middle aged man turned around with a concerned expression.

"I'm okay. I just broke up with my boyfriend."

"Well, he is not taking it very well." The driver laughed.

"No, it doesn't seem he is."

"Kick rocks, bitch!" Johnny was still raging as the car pulled away.

Suddenly, I felt as if a weight was lifted from my chest and I could breathe again.

24

The ocean breeze grazed my skin as I stood on the balcony of my hotel suite.

Since I was booking a room last minute the only vacancy was the beach house suite at a hotel in Venice Beach.

With the money I saved and the five million dollars from Sasha's trust, I decided to splurge and treat myself to a week stay.

I looked onto the beach and watched a few beachgoers laid out and basking in the sun. It wasn't that crowded out which was nice.

I sipped my wine and sat in the patio chair.

Out the corner of my eye, I saw a woman who looked like Sam. I leaned forward and realized it actually was Sam.

She walked alone on the beach wearing white shorts with a light blue and white stripped blouse tied at the front.

She did not walk in her usual confident stride. Her shoulders slumped slightly and she dragged her feet through the sand. I felt sad for her as I watched her walk onto the hotel patio. A hostess guided her to the beach bar.

Maybe I should talk to her?

I decided to take a chance. We were never really friends, but I owed her at least an explanation for everything that happened with Sasha.

I put on my yellow sundress and took the elevator down to the beach club bar.

She stared into a margarita glass then looked up and locked eyes with me.

I paused to make sure she would not attack me again and when a tear fell from her eye I decided it was safe to approach her.

"Hey." I sat on the bar stool next to her.

"Hey."

There was an awkward silence so I ordered a margarita.

"How are you doing?" I knew she was not doing well, but I needed to say something to her.

"Well, I'm sure you already know." She sighed and rolled her eyes upward.

"Sam, I'm sorry for how everything went down between us. It all just happened so fast." As soon as I spoke she looked up at me.

"Lexi, you had an affair with my husband. You were supposed to be my friend." She wiped the tear stain from her cheek.

"Let's be real, Sam. We were never friends. You had been using me since I met you. You never gave a damn about me." I took a sip of my margarita.

"Of course I gave a damn about you." She sat up facing me.

"Really, Sam." I looked at her from the corners of my eyes.

There was another awkward silence.

"Lexi, I do love Sasha." She looked up and I could see her heart breaking in her eyes.

"I believe you, Sam. But, you also love what he represents. And, by the way, are you happy with Craig?"

She paused for a second.

"He's good to me. I never gave it a real chance before."

I wasn't convinced.

"But, are you happy?"

"I mean, yes. Yes, I am." She stared down into her hands.

I could tell she was not sure. One thing I knew about Sam, she was always aiming for the brightest star in the sky and Craig was not it.

"Sam, you know. You never chose Craig."

She looked puzzled at me.

"When I met you at the Death of Love concert, you wanted to be with Luzar. But, then you settled for Craig. Then, you moved to Paris with Fred and left him for Sasha. Now, it seems you are settling for Craig once again. And, Craig is an amazing, talented person with a good head on his shoulders. But, is he the one you truly want to be with?"

I could not believe I was possibly convincing her to go back with Sasha since I was also in love with him. But, she needed to hear the truth and Sasha and I were likely never seeing each other again.

She was silent.

"So, why are you at this hotel? I thought you were back with Johnny?" She tried to change the subject.

"I left Johnny."

"What happened?"

"I knew it would not work out, so I left."

"So, have you seen Sasha recently?"

Her question made me reminisce about my time with him in the Skye. But, I decided not to reveal this and lied to her instead.

"No. Not since the media exposed us."

She set back and stared out at the beach.

"So, what are you going to do now?" She glanced at me then looked away.

The question brought back the fear of uncertainty in my future and if I could revive my career in the music industry.

"I don't know. What are you going to do, now?" I turned to face her.

"I don't know." She stared back at me.

We spent the remainder of our time together quietly sitting at the bar staring into our margaritas.

Part IX: Sam

25

I walked back to Craig's house on Venice beach and contemplated what Lexi said about me not choosing him.

Was she right?

With everything going on, he had been nothing but good to me.

As I approached the beach entrance to his home I noticed a shirtless man standing across the beach walkway staring at me.

His bald head was smooth and slightly pointed at the top, his tan skin was dry and cracked likely from constantly being in the sun. He tugged at the front of his blue swim trunks. As I walked closer, I realized he was rubbing himself from the outside of his trunks.

He stood grounded with his bloodshot eyes focused on me.

I paused for a split second looking around and realized there weren't many people around. Only a few who were too far away to witness.

My hands shook as I entered the code to the door of the tall barrier glass wall. I rushed in and quickly closed the door behind me. I turned around and through the glass the man continued staring at me and pleasuring himself.

I ran past the pool and into the back door of the house, set the security alarm, and closed the tan drapes blocking any light from the outside.

"Babe, there are a lot of crazy people in Venice Beach. I'm sure that guy is harmless and likely doing that to others."

Craig sat the restaurant bag onto the kitchen counter and pulled out the tacos and guacamole.

"It seemed like he was waiting for me." My hands were still shaking slightly as I pulled two plates from the cabinet.

I placed the plates next to Craig and he laid the food out, scooping extra guacamole onto my plate.

"Those guys get off on getting a reaction from people. If you ignore him, he will move on."

He grabbed both plates and I followed him into the living room to settle on the couch.

I was still shaken up and Craig wrapped me into his arms.

"Hey, I'm here. If you want me to beat that guy up, I will."

I smiled at the thought.

"No, don't beat him up."

"I will, cause no one jerk's off to my girl and gets away with it."

He kissed my forehead.

It was these moments that I loved being with Craig. He always knew how to make me smile.

"Okay, so which episode did we leave off on?" He grabbed the remote and clicked on the streaming channel.

"It was episode 5, they realized they were investigating

the wrong person."

I picked up one of my fish tacos and dipped it into my guacamole while Craig started the show.

26

"I've confirmed that you will receive your last deposit from the annuity next month. This is good because now you have a better idea of where you stand financially. The clothing and jewelry we will discuss in the negotiations with Sasha's board of trust. I don't see why they wouldn't let you keep your personal belongings. But, you need to find proof of purchase to show that you bought them."

David cleared his throat over the phone.

"Also, we need to discuss where you plan to reside permanently because this will determine the custody agreement. With Sasha being in a better financial position, dual custody will be your best option. That is if you can maintain a residence in or near Sussex."

The thought of me not seeing Sadie in so long brought tears to my eyes. I missed her little chubby face so much.

I wondered if she thought that I'd abandoned her.

"Did they say anything about me being able to do a video chat with her?"

"Yes. Sasha agreed to a video chat with your daughter this Sunday at noon. I will send you the details and link in an email."

"Okay."

"Samantha," David took a deep inhale, "let me give you some advice. I understand that you are with this new guy, Craig. But, if you want dual custody of your daughter, you need to be here. You need to be near her because the media is shaming you for being in Los Angeles with this man instead of here fighting for your daughter. You need to show some initiative."

"I'm just trying to figure everything out right now." Tears began to well in my eyes.

"I understand, but the world is watching you. Understand that public opinion can weigh heavily on your divorce. And, you don't want to be on the wrong side of that. I will have my assistant email you the information for your video chat with Sadie sometime today. Think about what I said, okay?"

"Okay. Thank you David."

I sat down the phone and stared out at Craig's small pool.

A notification chimed on my cellphone and I saw it was a news story on Sasha.

I forgot I had his name on my phone's notification setting to get updates on him whenever he was away.

I opened the link and there was a picture of a protestor pushing a cream pie into his face.

He was leaving an interview he did at a radio station and about fifty protestors gathered outside to protest his assumed sexual misconduct and toxic masculinity.

The article also stated that some of his endorsement deals were canceled because of the media scrutiny.

I felt sad that he was going through this after he worked so hard on his projects.

I wanted to console him, but with our legal separation

there was nothing I could do.

When I first stayed with Craig a few years ago, I thought his home was roomier than it seemed now.

The slim modern house sat so close to the neighbor's that I could look right into their backyard from the bedroom window.

And, Craig's minimalist Scandinavian decor was the total opposite of Sasha's grand opulence of priceless art, custom silk drapes and carpet, gold leaf crown moldings, and vintage furnishings.

I missed the accommodations of the estate with the spa and being topless outside at the pool with no care in the world. I didn't even have to clean anything.

After living in such luxury it was difficult to appreciate Craig's lifestyle.

I walked around each small room trying to see how I could make it feel more like home to me. I also needed to research some apartments I could rent near Sussex.

Constantly thinking of the divorce was exhausting, so I decided to spend some time by the pool to clear my mind.

I put on my sage green bikini, settled on the pool lounge, and watched the beach goers frolic in the sand.

As soon as I began to relax, out the corner of my eye I spotted the man from yesterday.

This time he crossed over the beach sidewalk and walked right up to the glass barrier wall. His eyes were so bloodshot I could not tell the color of his iris.

He grinned revealing heavily stained yellowish brown teeth.

Still wearing the same blue swim trunks he reached his hand down the front and revealed his large crooked manhood. He pressed himself against the glass and began humping on it leaving a smear behind.

I jumped up from the pool lounge chair and ran into the house grabbing my cellphone and calling the police.

After about an hour of waiting, Craig and the police finally showed up.

Craig showed them the security camera footage of the man.

They didn't seem care about what happened as they asked routine questions and sighed as if they had better things to do.

They promised to keep a look out for the man, but it was not convincing.

After they left, Craig was unusually quiet.

"Maybe we should put some outdoor curtains on the glass wall."

"Sam, I'm not putting curtains on the outdoor wall." His voice raised slightly.

"Why not? Everyone can see into the pool area and the house."

"Sam, no!" This time he shouted, making me stand back.

Shocked, Craig hadn't raised his voice at me since we got back together.

He sat down on the couch and stared at the floor.

"What's wrong?" I cautiously sat next to him on the couch.

"Sam, I was in a business meeting. That man cannot get in here. There is nothing that man can do to you. You are safe."

"What am I supposed to do? Hide in here forever or watch him climax all over the glass wall."

"Well, Sam you can start off by going back to work then you won't be here all day to see that man." He turned toward me.

"What do you mean?"

"Sam, you're being cut off from Sasha financially. You need to find an apartment in Sussex and have to fly back and forth monthly between here and there. All of this cost money. You have a home here, but you need to get yourself together financially and be more independent."

I sat back and stared at Craig.

"But, you have enough to take care of us both. You said you would take care of me." I felt my skin grow warm.

"Sam, you have a place to live with me always. I love you, but you spend a lot of money. I have enough, just not for your lifestyle expectations."

He turned away and leaned back on the couch.

"For example," He held out his hand and began counting on his fingers, "in London I spent over $5,000 on clothes for you. I have money but touring and writing music does not pay what it used to. I only got about $20,000 from the shows in London and a forth of that went to buying you clothes."

"Craig, you're worth millions of dollars! Are you really giving me crap about $5,000 right now."

I stood from the couch and stormed into the kitchen.

"Sam, that shit adds up! I have to think about retirement and future projects. I don't want to be out here touring myself to death each year to maintain an expensive lifestyle. And, we live a pretty good life that most people can't even dream of. You're just spoiled." He stood up and joined me in the kitchen.

"I'm not spoiled. You promised to take care of me and now you're trying to go back on your word." I crossed my arms and turned away from him.

"Sam, I will help you get an apartment because I know you want to be with your daughter, but you have to pay the rent and the plane fare. We have to work together on this. I even spoke with Joe about finding you some commercial work. He said advertising would be perfect and you can make thousands as an influencer on social media because you already have a large following."

I could not believe what I was hearing.

I did not want to sell products on my social media.

To think a few months ago I was in London, Milan, and Paris being paid by top designers to wear their designs on the red carpet and party with the most famous people in the world.

I tried contacting Renae several times about the upcoming fashion weeks for next year's Spring-Summer collections. But, without Sasha she did not see any value in continuing working with me.

I didn't understand until now how much I would have to sacrifice leaving Sasha.

I realized being with Craig was a mistake and wished for my old life back.

"Just think about it, okay?" Craig kissed my forehead then went outside with a towel and cleaning spray and started wiping the smear stain from the outside glass.

27

My hair flowed in the wind as I cruised along the Pacific coast highway.

I decided to rent a car and take a drive to clear my mind.

The thought of sitting at Craig's house and witnessing the pervert again was depressing me. So, I had a rental agency deliver a white convertible to the house so that I could get out.

The weather was perfect with a calm wind and the sun dancing on the waves below.

I was enjoying the drive so much that I didn't realize I was heading towards Sasha's Malibu mansion.

I slowly drove toward the neighborhood's gated entrance and saw the usual security guard sitting in the small guardhouse.

I still had a lot of my clothes and personal things there and I was technically still Sasha's wife so I decided to try my luck and pulled up to the gate.

My hands became cold and clammy as I handed the security guard my driver's license. I sat as calmly as I could as he scanned the back and looked intently at his computer screen.

He turned to face me and my heart skipped.

"Here you go. Enjoy the rest of your day ma'am."

He handed back my license and opened the gate.

A relief fell over me as I drove through.

Cruising through the meticulously manicured streets, I felt clean and above everything.

I used to love driving through here. It was as if I was transported to an another world. A clean, safe, and rich world.

Even the air smelled fresher and the wind blew gentler over my skin.

I pulled up to the white gate of Sasha's property and entered my code.

The gates opened revealing the white Mediterranean style mansion.

Parking in front of the large door, I almost tripped over myself rushing out of the car.

I entered my code for the door and when the green light lit up on the key pad, I was home free.

Although we had not been here for almost a year there was not a speck of dust or stuffiness in the house. The housekeepers kept everything in perfect condition.

Immediately, I walked to the glass wall that looked over the pool area and out toward the ocean.

I slid open the doors and the saltwater breeze swept over my body almost as if it were hugging me and welcoming me home.

I decided to spend the day here since Craig was busy with his band interviews to promote their upcoming European tour. And, after everything I went through with that creepy stalker that no one cared about, I deserved some peace.

After ordering food delivery from my favorite restaurant that was nearby, I put on one of my bikinis I left here in my closet, made a cocktail, and laid on a lounge by the pool.

It was complete privacy, no one could bother me or harm me here. So, I decided to take my top off and enjoy not having any tan lines.

I missed this.

Then, I remembered that soon all of this would be gone and one day Sasha would share this life with someone else.

I sacrificed so much and worked hard to make it here and now another woman would be living my life and taking everything from me.

What am I doing? Am I really giving up this lifestyle to be with Craig?

I remembered what Lexi said.

I never chose Craig.

She was right. I never pursued him. He was always pursuing me and I let my need for an ego stroke overcome what I really wanted.

I wanted to be with someone who was ambitious, a leader, the top guy that everyone wanted to be and be with. I wanted luxury, to travel the world and rub elbows with icons. And, I made it. I was living every girls' dream. I came from a poor upbringing and was on top of the world.

Craig was a good man, but he will never be the man of my dreams. Only Sasha achieved that.

And, I missed Sasha so much.

Even with the cheating and rarely being home, he was everything I ever wanted.

I wanted my family back.

I wanted my life back.

Tears streamed down my face as I imagined my daughter in England so far away from me. And, Sean bouncing from one reality to another then having me abandon him.

I had no idea if I even had a chance of getting back with Sasha after leaving him for Craig.

Taking another sip of my cocktail I decided I'd better enjoy this moment because it was likely going to be the last.

A cold breeze woke me and I realized it was dark out.

I fell asleep on the pool lounge chair.

Only the pool string lights were on as I stared out into the darkness of the ocean.

I rushed back into the living room and turned on the lights while searching for my phone. I knew Craig likely called worrying where I was.

I realized I left my phone in the bedroom upstairs when I changed into my swimsuit.

As I scurried up the stairs, it began to ring.

It stopped as soon as I picked it up. It revealed 12 missed calls and text messages from Craig. Then, I saw that it was after 11 o'clock at night.

"Where have you been? I finished the interviews early and you weren't here. I've been worried sick about you."

I walked past Craig as I entered the door and sat my purse on the kitchen counter.

"And, where did this car come from?"

He stood in the doorway and studied the convertible in the driveway.

"I rented a car and went for a drive up the coast. I texted you that when I was driving back."

"After 11 at night! Where did you go?"

Craig slammed the door shut and stood with his hands on his hips in front of me.

"I went for a drive, then stopped at my favorite restaurant in Malibu."

"What restaurant?" He squinted his eyes at me.

"Craig, it's been a long week and I did not feel safe with that creepy man walking around so I went out to clear my head."

I went upstairs to the bathroom.

Craig's feet pounded on the steps. I could feel him sitting on the bed outside the door waiting to continue his interrogation.

I reluctantly came out to find him sitting on the bed looking down at his hands.

"You know, Joe has been telling me to leave you. He says you're bad luck." He continued staring down.

I rolled my eyes.

"He said you ruined every man you've been with. And, maybe he's right. Your old fiancé in Georgia said in an interview he went to rehab because of you, Fred's career is ruined, Sasha is being canceled in the media for having a harem full of women, and even my band broke up for a time after I was with you the first time."

I stood still in front of him.

My heart ached knowing that this was it for us.

We were breaking up for good this time.

Now, I was really on my own.

Part X: Lexi and Sam

28

"We have now landed in Atlanta. We've enjoyed you during this flight. Enjoy your stay."

It felt good being back in Atlanta after all this time.

After my week alone in LA I realized I needed to come home and clear my head. And, my mom was nagging at me to visit her.

I walked through the familiar airport and felt at peace as I rode up the escalator with the large 'Welcome to Atlanta' sign with Atlanta landmarks and history icons painted on it.

I collected my suitcase from baggage claim and waited for my mom outside.

The thick, humid air was something I had to get used to again. It was so bad I'm sure the humidity made my edges curled up as soon as the plane landed.

BEEP BEEP.

My mom pulled up in her new SUV waving frantically at me with the biggest smile.

I missed home.

* * *

"You should buy a house here."

My mom sat across from me at the kitchen table after preparing a large southern style breakfast.

"A lot of big name celebrities are buying property here. And, I learned from your cousin, Ashley, that the music and movie industry is expected to blow up down here. It's the perfect place to start your own business. And, with your money you saved, you can get a nice home for a third of the price of what those Hollywood houses are going for."

I nibbled on my honey biscuit and contemplated moving back for good.

"Well, I did want to invest in some property. I could take a look and see what't out there."

I needed to figure out my next steps. While I could live off the five million dollars from Sasha's trust if I budget, I had goals and aspirations that I wanted to pursue.

"I already spoke to your cousin. You know she's a licensed real estate agent now. And, she is doing very well. She's gonna call you some time today."

"Thanks, mom."

"They don't build houses like this anymore."

Ashley opened the door of the dark blue 1920's craftsman style home in East Atlanta.

"This is a one-story, three bedroom and two bath, at 1200 square feet, on a 0.3 acre lot with an attached one car garage. The current owners added an in-ground pool and there's an in-law suite in the back you can turn into a studio for your music."

She was right, the home was well built with thick plaster walls, hardwood floors, and crown molding.

This was the third house we looked at and I immediately felt at home. I could see myself living here.

"What's the asking price?"

"Four hundred and thirty thousand dollars. We can negotiate the price but houses go really fast in this area."

"I'll take it. All cash with a 30 day closing."

The month went by so fast and the process was smoother than I expected.

I waved at the moving company as they drove away after spending hours moving the furniture into my new home.

I stood in the living room and looked around.

This was the beginning of my new life.

Knock. Knock. Knock.

Thinking one of the movers may have forgotten something, I opened the door to a mail carrier standing on the front porch balancing a large package on a hand truck.

"Ms. Lexi."

"Yes."

"I need you to sign here."

I noticed the large box was addressed from Scotland and I thought of Sasha.

The young man wheeled the package just inside the door.

My heartbeat quickened.

I hastily opened the box and settled in paper shavings was a leather trunk with a black envelop on top.

It was a handwritten letter from Sasha:

Dear Lexi,

Here is a case of my new Scotch that we tasted in Skye. Your mother gave me your new address. Congratulations on your new home. Atlanta is a great place for music and you will do very well. I spoke with some of my friends in the industry out there and they are eager to work with you. And, when all of this media attention calms down, I'd like to see you again one day.

P.S. The private detective found all of your jewelry and will be sending it to you soon.

If you need anything, I am always here.

Love,
Sasha

I held the letter to my chest and let the tears roll down my cheeks.

Knowing that I would see him again made me feel hopeful for the future.

I opened the trunk and retrieved one of the heavy amber glass bottles. There were two sniffer glasses like the one's Sasha and I used at the distillery.

Our names were etched into each glass.

I took the one with his name etched on it, poured some whiskey into it and tasted the smooth, sweetness of my memories with him.

29

I watched in horror as DJ discussed his new book about our relationship on an entertainment television show. He actually titled the book 'My Life and Heartbreak with Sasha's Wife'.

He was being represented by a woman from London named Veronica.

I kept hearing her name in the media as she was representing everyone who knew us.

I was packing my belongings to move out of Craig's home while he was in meetings when I overheard DJ's voice on the TV.

He looked like he lived a hard life with his sunken eyes and hollow cheeks. His frame was so thin he was swimming in his suit. It seemed he'd aged 10 years.

I wondered how much he got for this book.

The worst part about it was that my sister and ex-best friend, Sophie, added commentary to the book as well. So, they all were making more money off of me than I was.

Then, Veronica announced on the show a bombshell that Jani was now writing a book about her relationship with Laney, me, and Sasha, insinuating some love triangle that never existed.

I recalled her claiming on her social media that she was pursued by both Laney and Sasha.

She even said that I stabbed her in the back after she taught me how to be a wife to an icon like Sasha.

I could not believe how low these people I once called friends would go for fame and money.

I booked a room at a hotel in Malibu and wanted to get there in time to set up my computer for my video chat with Sadie.

I found a realtor in Sussex who also worked with renters to help me find an affordable apartment.

There wasn't much for me to pack since most of my things were at Sasha's estate in Sussex.

So, I sat on the couch and watched DJ's interview about me.

Craig asked me to wait for him to say one last goodbye. I only had two hours to get settled before seeing Sadie. And, my attorney told me that being late would be detrimental in my custody case.

As soon as the interview was over, I heard Craig enter the house.

He looked tired and irritable.

"Hey." He glanced at me then sat his keys on the kitchen counter.

I stood from the couch, put my duffle bag on my shoulder, and walked into the kitchen.

We stared into each others' eyes and a tear rolled down his face.

He wrapped me in his arms and kissed me deeply.

"I wish this would have worked out for us, Sam." He pressed his forehead against mine.

"I do too."

We embraced for the last time, then I walked out the door and to my rental car without looking back.

I sat on the firm bed in the small hotel room with my laptop open waiting for the video call to see Sadie.

When the call came I quickly accepted and was staring at Sasha on the other end.

I paused then noticed the background was the Malibu house.

He stared back at me.

"Sam. Can you see me?"

I nodded.

"I noticed on the security feed you came here yesterday. So, I thought I would fly out here with Sadie and Sean so you could be with them and for us to talk."

"Okay." I sat frozen in disbelief.

"Do you want to come over?" He stared directly into my eyes through the computer screen.

"Yes. I do." My breath deepened.

"Okay. We look forward to seeing you soon."

I ran through the hotel with my bag and into the rental car, almost knocking over the doorman.

I drove like a maniac as I rushed to the estate praying that this would all turn out good.

The security guard waved me in and I drove the familiar path to the mansion.

As I entered the property gate, Sasha was standing in the doorway.

I climbed out of the car and ran towards him with tears streaming down my face. He grabbed me slightly lifting me from the ground and held me in his arms.

I kissed him deeply and he kissed me back.

"I missed you." I cried out as he continued to kiss me.

"I missed you, too." His dark brown eyes were sad as he looked down at me.

"Mommy!" Sadie squealed as she ran to me with her arms outstretched.

Sean was right behind her and they both held onto each of my legs.

I bent down and kissed both their little cheeks as tears streamed down my face.

"I missed you both so much."

"I missed you too, mommy." Sadie squealed.

"I missed you, too!" Sean called out.

We all went inside and Sasha laid out food he ordered from my favorite restaurant.

Then, we sat at the table as a family.

After putting the kids to bed, Sasha and I went outside by the pool to talk.

As soon as we settled on the lounge chairs he removed my clothes and pulled me on top of him.

I felt him firm between my thighs and I took him inside of me.

Rocking my hips over his large muscular body he locked eyes with me and did not look away.

He reached up and rest his hand on the side of my face and I kissed the inside of his palm.

The pressure built up inside of me and the heat escaped through my skin as I came closer to climax.

Then, lightness filled my head and I reached complete ecstasy.

We ended up making love multiple times for hours as the sun set and the moon rose.

I laid in his arms staring up at the crescent moon thankful to have my family back.

"I heard about the book your ex is writing." He looked

down at me as he caressed my back.

"Yeah, it's so humiliating. I wish there was a way I could stop it." I thought about the amount of humiliation DJ's book would put me through.

"Don't worry my team is on it. That book will never see the light of day nor will Jani's book."

I sat up to face him.

"Really? Thank you." I kissed his cheek.

"And, I heard there was a stalker revealing himself to you in Venice Beach. I had a talk with the Sheriff and they got him, so you don't have to worry about that anymore."

This was why I loved him so much. He always protected me the way no one else could.

"By the way. Who is the Veronica woman representing everyone? It seems like she's targeting you." I looked up at him as he propped himself up on his elbow.

"Well, before I met you, her and I had a fling. She wanted us to become more serious and I considered it. But, I ended up falling in love with you in America. After you and I were married, she seemed okay with everything, but it seems maybe she wasn't. And, now she is taking her revenge out on me in the media. But, don't worry, my lawyers are on it."

He sat in deep thought for a moment.

"Sam, with everything going on with this tabloid media mess, I need you by my side. I know that I haven't been respectful and very careless, but I ask for your forgiveness. I know this life can be tough, and I cannot promise that nothing will happen while I am on tour, but I promise that I will take care of you and honor you as my wife."

He picked up his pants and pulled a black suede ring box from the pocket.

My eyes widened as he opened the box revealing my

wedding ring and a ring with large diamonds wrapped all around.

I held out my hand as he put the rings on my finger.

I teared up and kissed him.

"I love you. And, we will get through this together." He placed my hand over his heart.

"I love you, too."

We kissed and made love again under the moonlight.

This was my life. The life I dreamed of. The life I reached for and grasped. I no longer had to gaze upon the stars because I now lived amongst them.

The End.

Back Matter

Read the full series

Star Reacher

Among the Stars

Dust from Stars